5.00

# MY BROTHER'S KEEPER

Mesty's Book 2003

Vancouver B.C.

# MY BROTHER'S KEEPER

## BY MARION WOODSON

RAINCOAST BOOKS

*Vancouver*

Raincoast Books acknowledges the ongoing support of the Canada Council; the British Columbia Ministry of Small Business, Tourism and Culture through the B.C. Arts Council; and the Government of Canada through the Book Publishing Industry Development Program (BPIDP).

First published in 2001 by

Raincoast Books
9050 Shaughnessy Street
Vancouver, B.C.
V6P 6E5
www.raincoast.com

Edited by Joy Gugeler
Cover art by Ben Blackstock

1 2 3 4 5 6 7 8 9 10

NATIONAL LIBRARY OF CANADA CATALOGUING IN
PUBLICATION DATA

Woodson, Marion.
  My brother's keeper

  ISBN 1-55192-488-9

  1. Brother XII, 1878-1934?— Juvenile fiction. I. Title.
PS8595.O653M92 2001        jC813'.54        C2001-910858-3
PZ7.W8685My 2001

Printed and bound in Canada by Webcom

For Bill, Gwyn and Ian

"I know not. Am I my brother's keeper?"
— Genesis 4:9

# CONTENTS

# ·ONE

"Two weeks? And I'll get paid?" Sarah had said when her uncle called to ask if she would babysit her cousin, James, in late August.

"Yes, and it shouldn't be too hard," he'd said. "Your Aunt Trish has to go to Toronto on business, but I'll be home most of the time writing my newspaper column. Besides, it really is a lovely place."

He was right — it was lovely. Huge cedar trees surround the large, two-storey shingled house and you could practically dive off the front porch into the ocean. A small island stood just a stone's throw away, with a chain of four larger ones hugging the horizon beyond it. On the beach, an upturned old rowboat lay on a pile of driftwood and a sailboat was anchored in the bay.

She tilted her head to read the upside-down name

on the rowboat. *Brother Mary*. Odd name for a boat. Odd name, period.

"Hey, James," she called to her cousin, who was pulling a backpack from the trunk of the car. "Is that your rowboat?"

"Yeah. It was here when we moved in."

"And is the sailboat yours, too?"

"Naw. Neighbours'." He grunted as he yanked out the heavy pack.

"Here, I'll get that," she said reaching for it.

"It's OK. I've got it." He shouldered the pack and headed for the house. Ginger, the Baxters' dog, had been watching them. She sniffed at Sarah suspiciously, then followed James toward the house.

"My mom said I've got to treat you like a guest and do what you say."

Sarah laughed. "Well, you can just treat me like a cousin and I'll be sure to tell your mother you're no trouble. OK?"

"OK," James grinned. "Here, in that case, carry your own pack!" he said, dumping it on the ground.

Despite this, Sarah thought James was a nice enough kid, for a ten year old. His blond hair was short and curly and his dark-rimmed glasses magnified his blue eyes.

"Why is your rowboat called *Brother Mary*?" she

asked as they climbed the steps to the front porch.

"We inherited it. Some guy left it here when he took off a long, long, lo-o-ong time ago. They said he could hypnotize people and perform black magic and all kinds of other scary stuff." James ticktocked his index finger in a wide arc before his eyes, then sleepwalked like a mummy toward Sarah. "Before he came here, he sailed around the world. He was even captain of a slave boat. Dad said he had a reputation for whipping the slaves and tying barbed wire all around the gunwales so they couldn't jump overboard," he said, scowling.

"But who *was* Brother Mary?"

"I dunno. Anyway, do you want to sleep here or upstairs?" he asked as he opened the door to a screened room at one end of the porch.

"Cool! Here for sure." It was exactly like a beach house bedroom should be: old fishnetting filled with seashells, ocean-worn bottles, driftwood and dried seaweed covered one wall; the other three were built of cedar halfway up, then screened off with fine mesh to the ceiling. It was the closest you could get to sleeping outside without actually sleeping outside.

"There are shutters you can close if it rains or if you get nervous. Do you want me to ..." James was tapping on the screen.

"No, no. I like it like this," Sarah interrupted. "If it starts to rain you can show me how."

There was a set of bunk beds in one corner and a single cot in another, an old beat-up dresser with a blurry mirror, two kitchen chairs, an overhead light with a string hanging from it, a candle and some matches on a shelf and a tall wardrobe.

James whistled an unrecognizable tune as he watched her unpack.

A bell sounded. "That's Dad," he said, "on the back deck. Dinner's ready."

At the opposite end of the house Uncle Steve was standing over a gas barbecue, wearing an apron that said EAT YOUR VEGETABLES. The smell of salmon cooking in lemon juice and dill made Sarah's mouth water.

"This place is *huge*," she said.

"We like it. Quite a change from Toronto, but we thought it was time to get out of the fast lane and back to basics. As you know, after visiting you in Nanaimo, we decided on Vancouver Island so here we are."

"We're glad you came," said Sarah. "Mom says it's great to have her sister a half an hour away instead of six hours by ferry and plane."

"Besides," said James, "now Sarah can come and play while Mom's away."

"Playing" with James was not exactly what Sarah had in mind. "Keeping on eye on him" was more like it, but she was getting paid eighty dollars for the two weeks, so if she *had* to play games she guessed she could manage it.

"James, will you please bring the bread and salad?" His father pointed toward the kitchen with a spatula.

"Come on, Sarah," said James.

"James, I asked *you* to do it," said his father gently.

"But Sarah can help. Why do I have to do everything?" James stood with his feet apart and his hands on his hips.

Uncle Steve rolled his eyes and looked patiently at his son. "You're exaggerating, James. You don't *always* have to do it. And furthermore, Sarah is not here to perform household chores. Come on, be a gracious host."

"OK, OK," muttered James.

Ginger followed James in and out of the kitchen and then settled herself under the table by his feet.

"So James tells me this house used to belong to a guy who hypnotized people and sailed a slave ship," said Sarah.

Her uncle nodded. "Brother Twelve. Interesting story, although I don't know a whole lot about it, just what the neighbours have told me. He set up a colony in the late 1920s, convinced his followers that Earth was going to

collide with Aquarius and that this was the one place
they would be safe. Those who joined his Foundation
handed over their money and worked for nothing. In
the end, he and his 'friend,'" he made quotation marks
in the air with his fingers, "got away with the loot."

"Really? How?" Sarah asked incredulously.

"What's that word you said?" James interrupted.
"A queer something."

"Aquarius? It's a constellation, a group of stars. I'll
show you later on that map of the night sky you have
on your ceiling."

"But how did he *do* it?" asked Sarah.

Uncle Steve shrugged. "He convinced them he was
their saviour."

"The rowboat is called *Brother Mary*. What did that
have to do with it?" she asked.

"A woman named Mary something-or-other was
one of the first to join Brother Twelve's Foundation
— she donated a lot of money to the cause. Brother
Twelve made her one of the directors and called her
Brother Mary. Special disciples in the Aquarian cult
were called Brothers."

"Did he live in this house?"

"Apparently. He lived here some of the time, although
there were other buildings around and more over

there," he pointed out to the ocean, "on Valdes and De Courcy Islands. The little island in front is Round Island, the one toward the right is De Courcy and the bigger one beyond that is Valdes.

Many of these Gulf Islands had Spanish names because early Spanish explorers named them. Sarah had been to two of them — Gabriola and Galiano — but others, like the ones she was looking at now, had no ferry service.

Jagged spikes of forest green pierced the cornflower sky. Seagulls circled and swooped over sandy bays and sandstone bluffs as golden as the beach. Sailboats paraded their spinnakers, plowing tugs held a steady course. The islands seemed to be calling to her.

"Do you think we could go to one of the islands sometime?" Sarah asked.

"When we get a good calm day, I could take you and James in the rowboat. It's an old clunker, but it's quite seaworthy and we do have three good life jackets."

"Maybe I'll investigate this Brother Twelve — I'm an excellent spy," said James.

Sarah was sure he wouldn't be much help, but it would keep him out of trouble.

"In the morning James will take you over to meet the neighbours. They're a French Canadian family with two girls. The older one, Giselle, is around your age, fourteen," her uncle said as they sat down to a salmon feast. "The younger one is Dominique."

"She's eight and she's got red hair," said James.

After supper James and Sarah played three games of Snap. By eight o'clock a pale moon and one faint star glimmered in the sky. When James retreated to his bedroom, Sarah went out to explore the backyard.

The large lawn was surrounded by trees and wild shrubs. Tubs of flowers were placed randomly on tree stumps or on the few posts that remained of an old fence. There was a derelict building covered with vines in the southwest corner and what looked like an old wheelbarrow and some scraps of lumber stacked beside it.

The air was balmy. The forest resonated with muted sounds — nature's lullaby. She found a dark corner of the yard away from the lights of the house and sat down to watch the stars.

She lay back on the grass and stared at the sky. Suddenly she heard whispers, "HUSH!" and again, "Hush! Hush!" Sarah sat up and stared in the direction of the voice. Shadowy figures stood motionless behind the fence. She held her breath and leaned around the tree trunks partially blocking her view to get a better look.

The porch light caught the shapes for a second and she thought she saw men in fedora hats and women dressed in calf-length woolen coats, close-fitting bell-shaped hats and sturdy low-heeled shoes. They scarcely moved, as though afraid to make a sound.

Another flicker. A boy about thirteen years old wearing dark overalls and a long-sleeved shirt stood apart from the others.

Sarah stood cautiously and moved a few steps closer. Streaks of mist rose from the forest floor and weaved slowly through long strands of fuzzy green moss hanging from the trees.

She detected a faint trace of perfume. Lavender?

A clammy hand brushed the back of her neck. She gasped and spun around. Nobody was there. A puff of cold air assaulted her face.

Sarah raced back to the house and crawled into bed. She was being ridiculous — strange noises and smells — she'd let her imagination get the better of her. She listened to the surf, smelled the cedar and felt the soft breeze on her face through the unshuttered screens.

Despite her scare, she was glad she had come. There was something special about this place and the mystery of Brother Twelve only made it more intriguing.

At the sound of rustling Sarah sat up in bed. She strained to hear the sound again. Lazy winds riffled the trees. Gentle surf massaged the sand. The whirr of a bird's wings was there and then gone. Nothing else. Yes, there was — a distant ship's whistle called. But the rustling sound she had heard was not repeated.

*Maybe it's the dog,* she told herself — the doghouse was on the porch, but the sound had come from inside the room, near the cot in the corner. In the eerie half-light it seemed forgotten and lonely.

Sarah shivered, grateful to be sleeping in the lower bunk. She snuggled down under the quilt, hoping for sweet dreams.

# TWO

Lego pieces were scattered all over the living room by the time Sarah had had her shower the next morning. James was reclining on the floor building something he claimed was a slave ship.

"Why don't you pick those up and then take Sarah over to the Tremblays?" said Uncle Steve as he headed upstairs to his study.

"Do I have to? I'm going to use them later anyway," James protested.

"Come on, James, I'll help."

"Thanks, Sarah. When you see Mrs. Tremblay, will you ask her if she'll be home the day after tomorrow? I need to go to Nanaimo to do some research at the library and she offered to be on call while you and James are here alone."

After they had cleared the floor, James insisted

on gathering the necessary equipment for a day of sleuthing: an old tweed "slouch" hat of his father's with a button on top and a small brim in front, a canvas bag containing a magnifying glass, a mirror, an empty pill bottle full of flour to "dust for fingerprints" and a notebook and pencil.

On their way to the neighbours' house, they climbed down a low bank and walked along the beach. The tide was high, but they carefully picked their way among piles of driftwood and boulders.

"Who lives there?" Sarah pointed to a small, weather-worn building barely discernible in a heavy stand of fir trees. Smoke came from the chimney.

"Aw, a really old guy. He's ... you know." James drew circles with his forefinger at the side of his head. "I think he's got that old-timer's disease."

"You mean Alzheimers," said Sarah.

As they walked along, Sarah stooped to pick up a seashell, small pieces of driftwood and chunks of worn beach glass and stuffed them in her pocket.

"Come on." James was getting impatient. "You're taking forever."

"OK, OK. I'm just looking for stuff to glue on the base of the lamp I'm making for my room."

"Can't you do it tomorrow?" James quickened his

pace and clambered up the bank toward a white ranch-style house.

Two girls were outside. The taller one was sweeping a concrete patio, the other was waving a bamboo rake in the air, whacking at a tree branch. At first glance you wouldn't have thought the girls were sisters, they looked so different.

"*Allô*, James! *Je suis ici.* Want to help me rake?" called the younger one.

"Hey, Dom-neek," James said racing toward her.

"Grab this," she tossed the rake to him and started running in circles around the tree.

Dominique was a wild-looking child, short and sturdy, with ginger-coloured hair that bushed out like tumbleweed.

"*Bonjour*," the older girl called. "I'm Giselle. You're James' cousin, Sarah, right?"

Sarah felt a twinge of disappointment. Giselle was a few centimetres taller than she was and her dark straight hair was smooth and shiny. Her brown eyes gazed steadily from under thick black eyebrows, her shorts were pressed and her T-shirt was spotless.

"It's nice to meet you." Giselle offered her hand.

"Same here," said Sarah, taken aback by such formality. "How long have you lived here?" Pretty dumb question — for all she knew, the Tremblays could have lived here forever.

Giselle swept the patio debris onto a dustpan. "Three years," she said. "I miss Montreal — it was *merveilleuse* — but I guess it's nice here, too."

"Do you usually speak French?" She had to be breaking some sort of record for dumb questions.

Giselle nodded. Sarah turned to see what James was up to, to break the awkward silence.

James was up to the third branch of the tree. He had his magnifying glass in one hand and was leaning precariously out over a limb.

Sarah gasped. "James, be careful!" she yelled. She didn't want him to break an arm on her first day. "Come down from there!" she demanded.

"Aw, why? I'm just looking. Besides Dom-neek's way higher than me."

Dominique was higher all right, almost to the top as a matter of fact. "Is she allowed to do that?" Sarah asked.

"*Oui*. It's all right. She pretty well does what she wants. It's easier to let her have her own way than to make her behave," said Giselle with a shrug. She raised her voice. "Why don't you show James *la petite maison* you made, Dominique?" She turned to Sarah. "It's just beside the garden so we'll be able to keep an eye on them. Let's go sit on the porch."

Giselle spoke quietly, but as she talked Sarah learned that Giselle had an older brother, Marc. "It's spelled with a 'c,' not a 'k,'" she said. "He's sixteen and he has a summer job at Yellow Point Lodge."

"I've got an older brother, too," said Sarah. "He's married and lives in Vancouver. And I've got two sisters. One works in a bank and has her own apartment in Nanaimo and the other one still lives at home. She's taking drama at Malaspina College, and she says —" Sarah paused, struck a theatrical pose with her chin in the air and one hand on her hip and said in a phony lilting voice, "— the *theatah* is the only way one can *troo-ooly* express the nature of *humanity* and find the *essence* of one's soul." She placed a hand over her heart then, threw her arms up and closed her eyes.

Giselle laughed.

"I wouldn't take theatre if you paid me, would you?" Sarah asked.

Giselle shook her head. "No, it's not my thing, but it's OK for some people."

"For sure. I don't mean I don't *like* theatre. I just wish she wouldn't act like she *invented* it. What do *you* want to study? Do you know yet?"

"*Oui*. I want to be an architect."

"Great!" said Sarah. "I'm going to be an anthropologist and study different cultures and collect artifacts from all over the world. Hey, maybe you can design my house — not fancy, just a plain one with lots of shelves and nooks and corners for my collections. Are either of your parents architects?"

"*Non.* My father works for the telephone company and *Maman* teaches Grades 1 and 2 in the French Immersion program in Nanaimo."

"My dad works at the pulp and paper mill and my mother has a part-time job at the Multicultural Society. What grade are you in?"

"Going into nine."

"Me too! What's your favourite food?" asked Sarah, eager to keep the question-and-answer game going.

Giselle rolled her eyes as she thought. "I love strawberries, but I *hate* oysters. Yeck!" she grimaced.

"Yeah, me too! Especially *raw*. Some people just open their mouths and pour the slimy creatures down their throats." Sarah put her hand to her mouth and pretended to retch.

Giselle giggled at Sarah's pantomime, then stretched her arms above her head. "I wish they weren't so skinny," she said.

"What?"

"My arms. They're too skinny."

"Not as skinny as mine," said Sarah. They held their arms together to compare and decided that they were almost identical.

They had just discovered that they both liked mystery novels but disliked science fiction when a woman in shorts and sandals, with her hair clipped on top of her head, came out and introduced herself as Mrs. Tremblay. She was carrying juice and granola bars on a tray.

"Don't mind me. I thought you might like a snack. I'm glad you're getting to know each other. I'll be inside reading if you need anything," she said, disappearing as quickly as she had appeared.

Halfway through her granola bar, Sarah asked Giselle if she had ever heard of Brother Twelve. Giselle nodded as she drained her glass of juice. "I wrote a report about him for school last spring. It makes you wonder how people could have been so ... what's the English word?" Giselle rolled her eyes and frowned. "Gullible, that's it," she said.

"Why, what's his story?"

"Well, let's see. I have my report in my room. Wait here, I'll get it."

Giselle ran inside and returned a few seconds later with a thin binder.

"That's right, I remember now." Giselle began to read from her report. "He was born Edward Arthur Wilson in 1878 to a religious family in Birmingham, England. When he was a boy he was apprenticed to the Royal Navy and travelled all over the world. In 1902 he reached New Zealand where he married and had two children. Five years later they moved to Victoria and he worked on a coastal steamer on a route from California to Alaska. In 1912 he abandoned his family and boarded a ship bound for the Orient. He traveled in China, India and Egypt studying astrology and ancient world religions before moving on to France, Italy and finally England. By then he said he had begun to hear voices, one that Wilson said was called the twelfth Master of Wisdom. The Master instructed him to build a safe place because he said Earth was on a collision course with Aquarius. The twelfth Master named Wilson Brother Twelve, after himself, and dictated a manuscript that became Brother Twelve's book *The Three Truths* in 1926." Giselle crossed her legs and turned the page. "While in England, Brother Twelve created the Aquarian Foundation and began to recruit followers and collect money. He planned to return to Vancouver Island in 1927 and buy property. He did, purchasing land here at Cedar-by-the-Sea and building the house your Uncle lives in and other buildings on the land, including a House of Mystery where he could communicate with the Masters by going into trances. Brother Twelve began publishing a monthly magazine called *The Chalice* and sent it to members of his Foundation. He gained such a following that the money poured in and hundreds of people came to hear him preach. During his sermons he used hypnotism to convince them of his powers. He cast spells on people with his eyes and was said to make them believe every word he said. Those in the congregation gave him money and some women even fell in love with him. And just think, it all happened right here!" Giselle raised her arm and swept it across the front yard.

"Sheesh. That's bizarre." Sarah shuddered. "Did most of his followers come from around here?"

"No, from all over, but mostly the U.S. and England. He picked a few from his congregation to *live* at Cedar-by-the-Sea and be his disciples. He made sure they were from different cities so they wouldn't know each other. I guess that gave him a better chance of brainwashing them, or whatever it was he did."

"Yikes!" said Sarah. "I can't believe people would come from all over the place just to listen to him talk."

"Oh, he did more than talk. He could make fire

jump from his hands and he claimed he could hear through walls. He even said he could murder souls."

"Murder souls? What does that mean?" Sarah asked uneasily.

"He called up the image of a person he wanted to die and imagined they were standing in front of him. Then he would slash his hands in the air, as if he were cutting the person's body and cast a spell."

"That's it?"

Giselle nodded. "As far as I know. I don't know whether it worked or not."

"Well, I don't believe it," said Sarah emphatically. "People don't die because of that hocus-pocus. Although," she hesitated, "I do sort of wonder about witchcraft and black magic sometimes. You know ... sticking pins into dolls, and curses? But that's just superstition. If people do die it's just a coincidence. Don't you think?"

"Definitely," said Giselle.

Sarah had to know more about Brother Twelve, but she wasn't so sure she wanted to get into black magic rituals. Still, she was fascinated. How did he do it? Was he really that smart? What if it were true? What if he really did have supernatural powers? Fire jumping out of a person's hands? Soul murders? She had to find out for herself. "Are there any books about him?"

"There were a couple, but you can't buy them anymore. They're out of print. The library might still have them, though."

"Where was this House of Mystery, anyway?" Sarah leaned toward Giselle, confidentially.

"Well, if you believe Mr. Otis — he's the old guy next door, a bit absent-minded — it's on your aunt and uncle's property west of that big maple tree in the ravine."

"Do you think Mr. Otis really knows? James said he's pretty out of it."

"Yeah, sometimes he is. Sometimes he talks to me as if I'm somebody else and doesn't make any sense, but other times he's perfectly fine."

Giselle picked up a twig and started to draw in the dirt at the edge of the patio. "If this is the ocean," she said, drawing a wavy line, "and this is the house," she drew a square, "and this is the big maple tree," she drew a circle, "then this is it." She drew a smaller square.

"There?" Sarah touched the small square.

Giselle nodded and started to draw a horizontal line between the circle and the small square. "Brother Twelve actually walked along *this* beach, right here."

"What's that?" Sarah pointed to little crosshatches

Giselle was adding to the line between the maple tree and the small square.

"The fence. He put it up about thirty-five metres from the House of Mystery. His followers had to stay outside the fence while he went into his trances. Sometimes he stayed in there for a week. When he finally did come out, shaking and sweating, he told them what his Brothers wanted them to do." Giselle pointed to the sky with her stick.

*Could it have been the ghosts of Brother Twelve's followers Sarah had glimpsed the night before?* "When was all this?" Sarah asked, suddenly less certain it was all a hoax.

"In the late 1920s." Giselle shook her head. "I'm not exactly sure of the dates."

"Were any kids involved?"

"I think there were a few. Mr. Otis was just a kid then, but who knows for sure."

*I'll definitely have to talk to Mr. Otis,* Sarah thought. "Hey, maybe the remains of the House of Mystery are still back there, in the woods."

"I don't know, that was more than seventy years ago," Giselle said skeptically.

"Sure, but there's no harm in trying. Let's take a look. Stranger things have happened."

# THREE

"Can James and I, and Giselle and Dominique, take a look around the property this afternoon?"

"Sure thing, explore all you want," her uncle said. "I really don't know what's out there. Haven't had time to wander too far, what with all these deadlines. My editors are always giving me tight schedules."

"What are you working on?" asked Sarah.

"It's a geological piece about the formation of the islands. In fact, that's why I have to go to town tomorrow, to interview a geologist and get some books out of the library."

"If you have time, could you pick up a book about Brother Twelve for me?"

"I'll see what they have." He scratched his chin. "That reminds me, I've been meaning to do an article about the infamous Brother. Quite a lot has been written about him — in the newspapers, books on cults — but maybe there's a new angle. I'll give it some thought."

At one o'clock Giselle and Dominique arrived for the Mystery House hunt.

Sarah brought along a water bottle, a box of crackers and a bag to collect any "artifacts" they found.

"I think we should head west," said Giselle, a compass in one hand and a hand-drawn map in the other. She held out her arm, pointing in that direction.

The Baxter property was densely forested except for the cleared area around the house. But the trees weren't the problem. It was the undergrowth that slowed them down — salal, Oregon grape, wild barberry, honeysuckle, fallen tree trunks and a gazillion other kinds of prickly, spiky plants.

For the next twenty minutes they grunted, batted, scratched and swatted their way through the tangle.

"There's a path ahead," called Giselle. She was in the lead, with James, Ginger and Dominique next and Sarah bringing up the rear.

"A path? You're kidding," said Sarah. "Why would there be a path out here in the middle of nowhere?"

"It's probably a deer path, but it does seems to be heading more or less in the right direction." Giselle had stopped so that the others could catch up.

"Awesome," said James.

"Excellent," said Sarah.

"*Fantastique*," said Dominique.

Ginger stood with her ears cocked and stared along the path.

They studied the map. Giselle checked the compass and decided the path was their best bet.

"Hey, guys! Look!" Sarah stopped and pointed to the left. "There's the dead tree, right at the edge of the ravine."

The snag was at least thirty metres tall, its naked branches contorted and black.

"Witches' hair!" cried Dominique. She scrambled over the bushes, stood under the tree and grabbed strands of dry moss from its branches.

James was right behind her. "Gross," he said as he plucked the grey, weedlike tendrils.

"You use it to start a fire," said Dominique. "You know, *un feu de camp*." She scratched a mosquito bite on her cheek, leaving a smear of dirt on her chin. Her T-shirt was half in and half out of her shorts and her socks were wrinkled around her ankles. "Can we light a fire and burn the witches' hair?" she asked Giselle.

"*Pas aujourd'hui*," said Giselle. "We don't have the time and the forest is too dry. It'd be dangerous."

"Can we build a fort then?" Dominique ran to a carpet of needles beneath a big cedar tree and gazed up into its branches. "This would be a perfect spot."

"We'll see," said Giselle. "For now it's a good spot for a snack."

They sat under the tree and passed around the crackers and water bottle.

"It's so secret," said Dominique, her eyes darting into the bush.

"It's pretty inaccessible now, but I bet seventy years ago there was a well-worn path to this spot, if this is even the right place," said Giselle. She wiped her forehead with the back of her hand.

Ginger whined, walked along the path toward the dead tree and stood absolutely still.

An eagle sat on a jagged top branch, black against the sky. Its head moved slightly, then it spread its huge wings and flew away, screeching.

"Where do we go from here?" Sarah looked at Giselle, who was looking at the map.

"I'm not going anywhere," said James and flopped back on the ground. "I'm going to stay here to hunt for clues."

"You mean artifacts," said Sarah.

"What are they?" said James, sitting up.

"In this case, an artifact means anything that could

have been used by Brother Twelve. Some wood or nails from the House of Mystery. A coin, a bottle, a door hinge. Get the idea?" said Giselle.

"I think we should scout the area within, say, a ten-metre radius of that rose bush." Sarah pointed into the shallow ravine. "There aren't very many roses around here. Maybe it was *planted*, but has grown wild over the years."

"*Oui*, good idea," said Giselle.

James jumped to his feet, helped Dominique up and fumbled in his pack for his magnifying glass.

"I found some old wood," called Sarah a few minutes later. "Part of a fence, I'd say." She heaved a weathered two-metre rail up for the others to see. "There's another one here, as well."

"Good. Maybe that means we're getting close to something," said Giselle.

"Come over here!" yelled James. "I found Brother Twelve's tent." He was on his knees, pulling on a faded square of green canvas that was tangled under the brush.

"I'll pull," said Dominique, dropping to her knees beside him and grabbing the edge of the fabric.

"We need more help. Sarah, grab a corner!" James motioned with one hand. The canvas suddenly jerked free and James' glasses flew off as the two of them fell backward into the salal.

"My glasses! I can't see." He looked around blankly.

Dominique put her face close to his and teased, "What will you give me if I find them?"

"I'll give you one of my baseball cards."

"OK." Dominique lifted the glasses carefully off an Oregon grape bush, wiped them against the side of her shorts and handed them to him.

"Thanks," he said as he adjusted them over his ears.

The canvas was about the size of a tabletop and had brass grommets along one edge. "It *is* from Brother Twelve, don't you think?"

"Could be," said Giselle.

"I found another clue," James called excitedly, ten minutes later. He was waving a metre-long piece of thin wire. "This *is* a clue for sure, isn't it, Sarah?"

"Could be," she replied casually.

"How come they say 'could be' about everything?" he asked Dominique. "Why don't they say, 'James, you are a good detective'?"

"Awesome stuff, James." Dominique patted his back encouragingly.

"You're a big help," said Giselle. "Anything we find is a possible lead."

Twenty minutes passed but they hadn't found anything else that seemed unusual. They folded up the tarpaulin and left it and the posts under the tree. James was taking his wire home to make a walkie-talkie.

"Can I try it when it's finished?" asked Dominique.

" 'Course you can," said James.

The trip back was easier because they stayed on the deer path. Giselle stopped to check the compass every so often. She was sure they would come out behind Mr. Otis' garden fence. Then all they would have to do was cut across the corner of his property and get to the Baxters' yard.

"Can we start on the fort tomorrow?" begged Dominique.

"Sure," said Giselle. "Why not? Who knows what'll turn up in the process?"

"It'll have to be in the morning, though. We need to be home in the afternoon while my uncle is away," said Sarah.

"I'll get driftwood from the beach and I've got some pieces of rope," said James.

"Let's try to do it with nothing but rope and what-ever we can find in the bush. An extra challenge. OK?" said Giselle.

"Once it's built, can I bring things from home?" said Dominique. "You know, secret stuff."

"I s'pose," said Giselle.

"I'll make the sign," said Dominique.

"Sign? What do we need a sign for?" The others looked at her.

"A PRIVATE PROPERTY sign," she said.

"You don't even know how to spell it in English," said Giselle.

"James will help me, won't you, James?" said Dominique.

"Fine, but you'll have to find something to make it with, out there in the woods," Sarah warned.

Suddenly an old man stepped out onto the path in front of them. He had thin, wispy hair like threads of frayed white cotton and his face was as wrinkled and brown as an autumn maple leaf. His shoulders were so stooped that he appeared to be without a neck and his chin was almost resting on his chest. He peered at them sideways, then cupped one hand around his mouth and whispered in a raspy voice. "You're not allowed! Stay away!"

"Hello, Mr. Otis," said Giselle calmly. "It's OK. It's just us. You know Dominique and James and this is James' cousin." She touched Sarah's elbow.

"Hush! What did I say? You'd better mind or you'll be sorry. He'll find out." Mr. Otis looked around anxiously.

"It's all right Mr. Otis, we won't talk," said Giselle. "Who would we talk to, anyway?"

"Them two." He jerked his thumb in the general direction of the Baxters' yard. "Nobody's allowed to go near them. Nobody."

Their eyes followed his thumb, but there was no one to be seen.

"We won't say a word. Don't worry," said Giselle. She stepped closer to the old man and looked into his face.

"Giselle. Is that you?" Mr. Otis looked surprised. His face cleared and his expression changed.

"Hi, Mr. Otis," said James.

"*Salut*, Mr. Otis," said Dominique.

"We've got to get back now, but we'll see you later, Mr. Otis," said Giselle. "Don't forget to ring that old school bell or hang a towel on the tree in your front yard if you need anything, OK?"

"Yep. And thank you for the cookies you brought last time. Raisin, weren't they?"

"Yeah. I'm glad you liked them." Giselle smiled.

Mr. Otis waved goodbye and turned to go back to his house.

"See what I mean?" said Giselle as they continued. "He's a bit mixed-up sometimes, but then he snaps out of it."

"But who was Mr. Otis talking about? Saying we couldn't go nearer or 'he' would find out? Who is 'he'?"

"Search me," said Giselle.

"Do you think it has anything to do with Brother Twelve?"

"Maybe," she said. "If Mr. Otis really was here when all that happened."

"Well, let's ask him the next time we get a chance," said Sarah. "We need an excuse to go and visit him."

"Easy," said Giselle. "Cookies."

Sarah had intended to read in bed for an hour, but her book soon slipped from her hands and she drifted off to sleep.

Somebody was calling her name, softly, coaxing her. "Sarah. Sarah."

She sat bolt upright in bed. It was pitch dark and what was that smell? Some kind of flower?

"Who's there?" she whispered.

She sensed rather than saw movement near the cot. Over the sound of the surf she heard a moan, followed by creaking bedsprings and footsteps at odd intervals, as if someone was limping.

She tried to speak again, but her throat was dry and her heart was racing. She had a metallic taste in her mouth. She held her breath to listen.

A sudden thump. She clapped both hands over her mouth. A yawn. More thumping.

Ginger! The Baxters' dog was outside on the porch. Sarah got up to call Ginger into her room, but the dog would come only as far as the door; she would not cross the threshold.

Moonlight shone through the screen filling the room with a silvery light. Sarah walked around the room touching the dresser, the chairs, the wardrobe, the candle, the old bottles in the fishnet. She got back into bed, resolving to close her shutters tomorrow night. Just in case.

# FOUR

The next morning when they met at the maple tree, Sarah was not surprised to find that Giselle had drawn up a plan for the fort.

"I couldn't do it *exactly*, because I'm not sure what kind of materials we'll be able to find, but this will give us an idea, OK?" she said.

"It looks perfect," said Sarah.

"Do you think the Egyptian hieroglyphics are too much?" Giselle pointed to a vertical row of images she had sketched on each side of the entrance.

"No. I think they're mysterious. Where did you copy them from?"

"From a book I borrowed at school about ancient Egyptian religion. The kind that Brother Twelve studied. It can be our trademark."

Sarah considered telling Giselle about the strange

sounds she had heard last night, but now they seemed distant and unimportant. The air smelled of wild honeysuckle and spicy dried seedpods; the sky hummed with birdcalls and insects. Good omens.

James brought two pieces of yellow nylon rope, salvaged from the beach, and a flat piece of driftwood.

Dominique brought part of a torn lace tablecloth, a pink plastic vase and an assortment of seashells.

"You'll have to take that stuff home when we leave," said Giselle. "Plastic and lace are *interdit* here." She turned her attention back to the plan. "So, first things first. We have to find the right spot. The ravine would be best, because the cliff could form one wall, and then we would just need to find two trees that we could tie a pole between to form the other three. We could lay branches for a lean-to roof and prop stuff against the sides," Giselle blurted enthusiastically.

"Pole? What pole?" James looked puzzled.

"That is the challenge," said Sarah. "We have to find one. We hunt for a fallen tree, trim off the branches and — presto! — we have a pole."

"OK, I accept your challenge. Let's hunt," said James to Dominique.

"*Un moment.* First we have to find just the right place. The trees need to be close enough together to be the proper dimensions." Giselle looked around.

"And we have to get the right-sized pole. About six centimetres across, eh, Giselle?" Sarah made a circle with her thumb and forefinger.

"Right," said Giselle.

"Let's walk toward the dead tree," said Sarah heading in that direction. Ginger snarled. "What's the matter, girl?" The dog was standing stock-still with a front paw raised, her tail straight.

"Come on, it's OK. The eagle's not here today," coaxed Sarah, but Ginger would not move. Her nose seemed to be lined up with one of the lower limbs. Sarah moved closer and Ginger whined. Something was wedged between the branch and the tree trunk. At first Sarah thought it was a twig, but then realized it was too smooth — it was a braided leather handle of some kind. Ginger gave a yelp and ran down the path with her tail between her legs as Sarah hurried back to show Giselle.

"That's weird," said Giselle. "I wonder what it was used for?"

"A genuine artifact," Sarah said, putting the leather handle in her pack, and they got back to the fort building in earnest.

They found the perfect spot — a grassy area against one wall of the cliff exactly two metres across. Giselle had brought a tape measure, of course. There were two trees also almost two metres apart and parallel. It would provide a cozy nook, sheltered from the afternoon sun, but would it be large enough for the four of them and a dog?

"As long as James and Dominique can fit, we can stay outside and stand guard. We'll just take turns if it's too small," said Giselle.

The forest floor was littered with dead trees and broken branches. Many of the trees had, through the years, turned into "nurse logs," and a huge variety of new life had taken root: fungi, mosses, weeds, seedlings, vines, wildflowers and shrubs were flourishing in the decaying remains of the tall giants.

It took some doing to find a tree that was the right size and sound enough to support the weight of the roof. They pried, grunted, hauled, lifted and yanked until they managed to salvage a reasonably good one. Meanwhile Ginger slept in a shady grotto in the bushes.

"Looks like Ginger's found herself a deer's bed," said Giselle.

"Is it lunchtime yet?" asked Dominique.

"No, but we can have a rest, a cookie and a drink." Sarah unzipped her pack.

"What kind of cookies?" asked James.

"Guess."

"Cream puffs," said James.

"James, cream puffs are not cookies. I made you peanut butter because I thought they were your favourite."

"They are. They are. Thank you," said James, taking an enormous bite.

By eleven-thirty Sarah and Giselle had managed to whack off the branches and break off the top of the dead tree, leaving a two-metre length.

"You know, this could be the very spot where Brother Twelve had his House of Mystery. I wonder what it looked like?" Sarah said.

"I saw a picture once. It was tucked into the forest and had only one room. The front door and two window frames were painted white." Giselle was trimming the branches, measuring them and placing them in two piles — one for the roof, the other for the walls.

Giselle was thinking out loud. "The Egyptians built pyramids to be used as tombs for the Pharaohs, whose bodies had to be preserved for eternity. They also believed in making human sacrifices there, mostly slaves or prisoners-of-war or servant girls who were killed and put in the tomb with the dead Pharaoh, to serve him in the afterlife." Giselle looked thoughtful for several seconds. "Brother Twelve did his share of sacrificing, too."

"What do you mean? Who did he sacrifice?" Sarah stopped what she was working on and stared at Giselle.

"Oh, he had ways of getting rid of the people he didn't want around. He didn't exactly kill them, but he would threaten to kill their souls, or send them to Ruxton Island without any food. His followers renamed Ruxton Devil's Island and at least two people went there and never came back. He even tried to convince some to kill themselves, if they'd run out of money or were too feeble to do hard work."

"Did you see any pictures of these places? Besides the House of Mystery, I mean."

Giselle nodded. "I think the house your uncle bought is the one he lived in. He also had a Centre Building nearby where his office and meeting hall were located. It was lavish — a huge place with a veranda and sloping windows and it had offices, hardwood floors, four upstairs bedrooms and a big assembly hall. That was where he lectured, for hours at a time, if you could call them lectures." Giselle finished measuring a branch, eyed it for straightness and tossed it on one of the piles.

"The buildings on De Courcy Island where the followers lived were plain, unpainted sheds. Some even had dirt floors," she continued. "There were five forts made of rough cedar with no windows or doors. People had to get in through trapdoors in the ceilings. The forts were stuffed with rifles and ammunition. Brother Twelve was paranoid, afraid somebody would steal the gold."

"Did you say gold? Where did he get gold?"

"He took the money people gave to the Foundation and got it changed into gold coins at the bank. Then he put the coins in jars, covered them with melted wax, put them into boxes and buried them on De Courcy Island. Naturally, that meant the whole island had to be guarded. They put up signs and fired shots to scare strangers away." Giselle sat down and rubbed her shoulders.

"Maybe he learned how to make people do what he wanted when he worked on the slave ships," said Sarah. "James said he used to do that."

"I wouldn't be surprised," said Giselle. "The guy traveled all over the world, could speak lots of different languages and he was a very good sailor. His boat was called *The Lady Royal*."

Sarah plunked herself down wearily beside Giselle. "I'd like to go to De Courcy or Valdes, just to see what's left."

"Maybe Marc could take us over in the boat on his next ..." Giselle stopped mid-sentence.

Dominique had persuaded James to leave his sleuthing equipment behind and help her gather fallen branches for the roof. At least that's what they were supposed to be doing. Instead they were enthusiastically gathering a huge pile of dry twigs and dead branches.

"Psst, psst ... *un feu de camp*," whispered Dominique.

"Sorry. No campfires. The woods are too dry. It's against the law," said Giselle.

"Aw, come on," said James, throwing a branch over his shoulder.

"It's OK," said Giselle. "We can use the dry branches another time. We'll have a campfire on the beach one of these days instead."

Reluctantly James and Dominique turned their attention to decorating — that is, gathering flowers.

By twelve o'clock the pink vase, full of wildflowers and weeds, was sitting on a stump, James was examining a small chunk of wire under his magnifying glass and Dominique was serving James "tea" in arbutus-leaf cups from a cedar bark teapot.

Giselle and Sarah had tied the pole between the trees and had laid several of the larger branches between it and the cliff. The sun was directly overhead, blazing hot.

They would have to call it quits for the day. They made a list of things to bring tomorrow and headed home.

"I didn't make the sign," wailed Dominique before they had gone very far.

"I know. We didn't have time for the artistic touches today. Don't worry, you can do it tomorrow, or the next time we come." Giselle consoled her.

"Shhh. I can hear whistling," said Sarah. They stopped to listen.

"Marc!" Dominique raced up the path, yelling at the top of her lungs. "Marc! Marc! *Viens ici. Nous sommes ici, dans le fôret.*"

By the time the whistler came into view, he was carrying Dominique on his shoulders.

Marc stopped on the path and looked at them. He was their brother all right, half Giselle and half Dominique. He had Dominique's blue eyes and red hair, Giselle's tall, slim body and solemn-looking face and a smile that started out like Giselle's — slow and hesitant — and then turned into Dominique's impish grin.

"Marc, this is Sarah," Giselle said.

"Pleased to meet you." He nodded formally. "Dominique, you'll choke me." He tilted his head back and loosened her grip on his neck.

Sarah realized she had been staring and that she

hadn't acknowledged the introduction. "Pleased to meet you, too," she muttered.

She was suddenly very aware that her hair was as tangled as the forest undergrowth, thanks to the branches and wind. Her legs and arms were scratched and dirty and her shorts were stained with salal berry juice.

He looked her up and down and grinned. "*Tu as des beaux cheveux*," he said.

She was really flustered now. Why was he talking about horses? She quickly answered him in French. "*Non, je ne suis pas un cheval.*"

The others started laughing.

"He said he likes your hair," murmured Giselle. "Marc likes to tease."

Her hair! And she had said 'No, I am not a horse.' Sarah tried to laugh it off, but her face was flushed. "We'd better get home, James. Your dad will be leaving soon," she said, hurrying along the path with a backward wave.

"Marc, would you take us to De Courcy Island sometime?" Sarah heard Giselle's voice behind her, but she didn't hear Marc's reply.

# FIVE

By one-thirty Uncle Steve had left for town and Sarah had had her second shower of the day, combed her hair, put on clean shorts and her favourite T-shirt and slathered her face, arms and legs with sunscreen. For the first time since she had arrived at Cedar-by-the-Sea, she leaned close to the blurry mirror in her room and studied her reflection.

Plain. Plain, straight, shoulder-length brown hair. Plain bangs. Plain, round face. Plain eyebrows arching over plain, hazel eyes. Plain chin, plain cheeks. Not a dimple or freckle or even a mole to relieve the plainness.

Giselle and Dominique came over with their mother to ask if Sarah and James could go swimming, so they left a note for James' dad and headed down to the beach.

The water was perfect: cold enough to refresh, warm enough to relax. Sarah lost track of time as she floated on her back, forgetting to worry about whether her arms were too skinny or whether or not she would have more strange dreams.

As they came out of the water, Giselle waved to her mother, who was reclining on a canvas lawn chair, reading a book. James and Dominique were building a sandcastle.

Sarah and Giselle spread their towels in the sun.

"I don't understand how a man like Brother Twelve could get so many people to believe he was their saviour," said Sarah as she lay down on her back.

"It happens in cults. You hear about it all the time."

"What do you know about cults?" Sarah rolled over onto her stomach and propped herself up on her elbows. "What makes people join them in the first place? What makes them stay when the going gets rough?"

"I don't know much, just what I read in the paper." Giselle's voice sounded sleepy.

"I'll ask my uncle. He's got filing cabinets a mile high. Maybe he'll know something."

"Mmm-hmm."

"Uncle Steve mentioned a woman who escaped with Brother Twelve. They took all the money. What was her name?"

Giselle revived a little and looked thoughtful. "I read a story about her at school. I remember it said her real name was Mabel Skottowe, but Brother Twelve renamed her Zurah De Valdes and then christened her Madame Zee, for short."

"What was she like?"

"She had red hair and had been married twice. The last time was to a rich man named Roger Painter who had been a stage hypnotist interested in magic and the occult. I guess she was very good at manipulating men. She was not good-looking, but she knew how to use her charms to get what she wanted."

"She sounds like a good match for Brother Twelve," said Sarah.

"She was. Brother Twelve invited Madame Zee and Roger to the headquarters here as favoured disciples. Brother Twelve claimed to have worked with him in a previous life."

A scream from Dominique brought them both to their feet.

James was laughing as he and Dominique took turns smashing the sandcastle with rocks. "Here comes a meteor," he yelled, holding a fist-sized rock over his head.

"They've gone totally ballistic," said Sarah.

Mrs. Tremblay looked up from her book, shrugged and smiled. "Ignore them," she said. "They're just trying to get a rise out of you. *Ils essaient de t'agacer.*"

Giselle said that Marc had agreed to take them to De Courcy Island on Saturday to see if they could find any of Brother Twelve's properties. "If it's OK with your uncle," she said.

"Uncle Steve said he would take us in the rowboat, but it would be nicer if we could all go at the same time," said Sarah.

"*The Long Trick* holds eight people, so there's plenty of room. *Maman* said she would come, too."

"Is that the name of your sailboat, *The Long Trick*?" asked Sarah.

"*Oui*. Marc named her," said Giselle. "It's in a poem by John Masefield called 'Sea Fever.'"

They dozed in the sun for half an hour and by then it was three o'clock, so Sarah thanked Mrs. Tremblay for inviting them and she and James left for home.

Giselle and Sarah agreed to meet at Mr. Otis' house at four-thirty to deliver cookies. They planned to listen carefully to the old man's conversation to try to sort fact from fiction. Uncle Steve wasn't home yet, so James came along.

Halfway there, Sarah stopped dead in her tracks.

A chunk of cardboard attached to a tree read: SARAH BEWARE. "That's creepy. James, you put that there, didn't you?"

"I did not. I don't even have any paint that colour," he said, exasperated. "I get blamed for everything. That's not even my printing."

"If you didn't do it, then who did?"

"I don't know. What do I care about a dumb old sign, anyway?"

"But that's *my* name, see?" Sarah ran her finger under the crudely painted letters. "It says SARAH BEWARE."

"Big deal," said James and shrugged.

"Big deal? How can you say that? How would you like it if it said JAMES BEWARE?"

Sarah decided to show Giselle the sign after the cookie delivery.

They climbed up from the beach and approached Mr. Otis' house by way of a path through the trees. Giselle and Dominique greeted them at his front door and Dominique knocked on it, hard.

They could hear Mr. Otis' quavery voice and shuffling footsteps inside. "Hold your horses, I'm coming," he said as he opened the door.

"Hi, Mr. Otis," said Giselle with a smile. "We brought you cookies."

"Leona! What are you doing here?" The old man held the screen door open and looked around furtively. "I can't talk to you," he whispered urgently. "None of us are allowed to talk to you. Mary neither. It's too risky to be doing this. He'll find out. You mark my word; he'll find out." Mr. Otis shooed them away with his hand.

"It's OK, Mr. Otis. It's just me, Giselle. We brought you some cookies." Giselle patted his arm and he quickly backed off and banged the door shut.

"Go away," he said, leaning his face close to the screen. "I don't want to go to Devil's Island."

"Of course you don't. We're your friends. Don't worry. We just came over for a visit. And to bring you these." Giselle reached for the plastic container Sarah was holding.

"Where did you get them? Did you steal them from the kitchen? He's the only one who can have them."

"Who?" said Giselle.

"The master. Now go away. He'll find out."

"Mr. Otis, look at me. It's Giselle." She stepped close to the door and smiled broadly.

Something passed over his features and he seemed to snap out of it. "Well, so it is. Have a seat." He opened the screen door, made his way slowly to an old rocking chair and lowered himself into it.

Sarah sat on the bench, while Giselle handed him the cookie container.

"I hope you like peanut butter cookies," she said. "Sarah made them."

"That's just fine. I've been crazy about cookies since I was a boy." He chuckled and nodded at James.

"They look good," said James, eyeing the container hungrily.

"Do you want one, son?" Mr. Otis asked.

"Yes, please and one for Dominique, too."

"Then that's what you shall have." Mr. Otis passed around the cookies.

"That was quite a while ago, when you were a boy, wasn't it?" said Giselle.

"It was. I was twelve or so when we came here."

*Twelve or so?* The boy Sarah imagined she saw on the first night at Cedar-by-the-Sea would have been about that age.

"What kind of clothes did people wear in those days?" she asked.

"Respectable ones!" said the old man testily. "Not like nowadays, people prancing around half naked."

"You mean the women wore stockings and long dresses?" said Sarah, drawing an imaginary circle around her legs to indicate the hem length.

"Yep."

"Did Leona wear clothes like that?" asked Giselle.

"They all did. The men wore overalls and long-sleeved shirts and proper boots."

"Do you remember Leona's last name?"

"No. She was friends with Mary, I remember that much. The two of them got into some bad trouble. 'Course getting in trouble was easier than falling off a log." Mr. Otis shook his head and drifted off — first in memory and then in sleep.

Giselle said he did that all the time, so the three of them slipped out but as soon as they were out of earshot, Sarah blurted her theory.

"I had a dream the first night I arrived. People were standing by a fence and they wore clothes like the ones Mr. Otis described. There was a boy with them, about twelve or so. Everyone seemed to be afraid. The other day Mr. Otis said not to talk to certain people and just now he said that only the master could have cookies. He said it was easy to get into big trouble. Leona and Mary did."

"Do you mean you think you *dreamt* what Mr. Otis actually *lived* as a boy more than seventy years ago? How could you know all that? Are you imagining it or is someone trying to tell you something?"

"Speaking of which, look at that sign!" Sarah said breathlessly.

Giselle frowned. "Looks like it was made by a little kid," she said, puzzled.

"Don't say that!" said James, who had jumped up on a log, balancing with outstretched arms. "Kids don't print like that, with the letters all squiggly."

"The sign can't mean me. There are lots of people called Sarah, after all."

"I bet it do-o-oes," taunted James.

Sarah took a package of ground meat from the fridge, mixed it with chopped onions, breadcrumbs, an egg, ketchup and Worcestershire sauce and put it in the oven to cook. Then she peeled potatoes and carrots and set the table for supper while James read to her.

"Mmm, smells good," said her uncle as he came in.

"Just meat loaf," said Sarah. She turned up the burner under the potatoes.

"How was your afternoon?" He dropped his brief-case on a chair and took off his jacket.

"Great," said Sarah. "We left you a note and went for a swim with the Tremblays."

"I wish I could have joined you, but I dropped in to the lawyer's office to pick up documents to do with our property and we got talking about Brother Twelve. Oh, by the way, I found a book about him for you at the library. Anyway, the lawyer told me about a court case — one of the disciples had been promised money for bookkeeping so he took what he thought was his out of the funds and left the colony. Brother Twelve charged him with theft, won the case and shortly thereafter the bookkeeper disappeared."

"Disappeared?"

"That's what they say. Other people who had worked for nothing despite a promise of payment testified in court, but Brother Twelve denied ever making such promises and 'cast a spell' around the courtroom with his 'magic eye.'"

"What happened?"

"Witnesses collapsed and the defence lawyer became disoriented and forgot what he was saying. The other disciples were terrified of Brother Twelve's power and were afraid to testify. But, and this is a very interesting example of the old adage 'fight fire with fire,' the prosecuting lawyer convinced them that he had powers, too — stronger and older than Brother Twelve's. The prosecutor gave each witness a Haida lip ornament to carry when it was his or her turn to testify. They were worn by Haida women as a sign of beauty, but the lawyer said this particular one had been the personal possession of a wise woman, a healer."

"And it worked?"

"Apparently."

"Do you know what it looked like?" asked Sarah.

"It was a smooth, crescent-shaped stone of some kind that would easily fit in the palm of your hand and it had a groove in it."

"I suppose anything can seem magical if enough people believe in it."

"I'll tell you one thing, Brother Twelve was a charlatan — a liar, a cheat and a thief. He was evil, but he fooled everyone. If you met him today, you wouldn't know what he was capable of, but he would make you uncomfortable. Not that you'd *want* to meet him."

"Well, maybe not him, but I am curious about the colony. Giselle said her brother would take us to De Courcy on Saturday, if it's OK with you. You're invited too. It might be useful if you write that article."

"Well, it's nice of the Tremblays to include me. I would like to go, if I can get enough work done by then."

"That reminds me, we found something I want to ask you about."

When she handed him the leather handle, he examined it and shook his head. "I don't know what it's from unless it's part of a harness or a bicycle handle, maybe some sort of tool. It looks quite old. A lot of things were made of leather then, before plastic and nylon."

"Do you think it could have anything to do with Brother Twelve?"

"Anything's possible."

# six

By nine o'clock Sarah was sitting on her bed making a list of the things she had heard about Brother Twelve:

- He sailed a slave ship.
- He traveled all over the world.
- He started a colony at Cedar-by-the-Sea.
- He talked people into handing over their money.
- He changed the money into gold coins.
- He claimed to be a Master of Wisdom.
- He built a House of Mystery, where he fasted and went into trances to communicate with his eleven Brothers.
- He could make fire jump from his hands.
- He could hear through walls.
- He escaped with Madame Zee and all the money.
- He cast a spell around a courtroom with his evil eye.

When she was finished, she turned to the index in the book her uncle had picked up from the library to see if it mentioned the leather handle she had found. She looked up "horses," "harnesses," "bicycles" and "tools." Nothing.

Sarah closed her shutters, decided they didn't make the room look cozier or safer, and opened them again. She lay in bed and thought of Giselle and Marc and De Courcy Island until she fell fast asleep.

She was awakened by the smell of flowers. A man with a short, pointed beard stood beside the bed, bathed in a soft blue light. She did not feel afraid. She knew him. He was her master. He was wearing a brown monk's habit with a red carnation pinned to the cowl, and stood with both hands extended. His eyes pulled her toward him.

"Sarah, Sarah," he called in a soft, seductive voice.

Sarah sat up, mesmerized by his unblinking gaze.

"Come with me, to the boat," he coaxed.

"Yes." Sarah rose slowly from her bed and drifted toward the door.

She heard a growl and felt something soft and wet

touch her hand. She was outside on the porch and the monk was disappearing into the fog near the beach. She must catch up to him! But she couldn't move. As she reached behind her, she felt Ginger's moist muzzle. Sarah came to her senses with a jolt.

"Ginger." She crouched beside the dog, stunned to find herself on the front lawn. Sleepwalking. She hadn't done that in ages.

A sharp crack, like a pistol shot, followed by a whistling whine echoed and re-echoed in her ears. She ran back to her room and dove for the bed, yanked the covers over her head, her heart pounding. She was freezing cold. She lay shivering for what seemed like an eternity until finally she heard Ginger yawn and roll over and Sarah forced herself to do the same. She slept fitfully until morning, dreaming about the billowing robes of a monk chasing her with a sign that read COME WITH ME.

Giselle phoned early the next morning. "I don't think I can go to the fort today," she said regretfully. "The blackberries are ripe and we usually try to get as many as we can for jam. Do you want to join us?"

"Sure," said Sarah. "Where do you go to pick?"

"There are good spots on your uncle's property. Do you think he would mind?"

"I'm sure he wouldn't. I'll ask."

When Giselle and Dominique came over an hour later, they headed out by the old shed, the smell of ripe blackberries drawing them closer.

They were wearing long-sleeved shirts, jeans tucked into socks and gloves for grabbing the thorny branches. Empty coffee cans swung on twine handles from their necks and Giselle carried a large, plastic pail.

"I'm not going any closer," said James. "I don't like bees."

"Where are the bees? I don't see any bees," said Giselle.

"Listen. Can't you hear them?"

"*Oui*, I can hear a few yellow jackets, but that's nothing. They won't hurt you if you don't make them mad," said Dominique.

"I think they're mad already," he said, hunching his shoulders and crossing his arms protectively in front of him. He walked toward the shed door. "I'll look around here instead."

"What's in there?" Sarah asked James.

"Junk, mostly. Me and Dad went in once, but we didn't have time for a good look."

Sarah unlatched the door and pulled it open.

It looked safe enough. There were a couple of old wagon wheels, a greasy engine, a ladder with two missing rungs, a rusty pitchfork with a broken handle and a workbench piled with old lawn chairs, a washtub, bicycle tires, oars, a small filing cabinet, a tackle box, broken toys, galvanized pails and aluminum saucepans of various sizes. Wooden and metal pieces of farm implements leaned against every square inch of wall space.

"We can use that ladder to reach the higher vines," said Giselle.

They carried it out and began to pick.

"What is this thing, Giselle?" called James. He was tugging something away from the assortment of old lumber. It looked like a wheelbarrow, except it was just handles and a frame with two sturdy boards about thirty centimetres apart. Several heavy-duty bolts and screws were attached.

Giselle turned to look. "Where did you find it?"

"Right there beside the shed." James pointed.

"It's a plow. See the end of it? A shovel-like thing was attached to that frame and used to plow the ground for planting."

"But where did they hitch up the tractor?" asked James.

"They didn't. They might have hitched horses or oxen, if they had them. People often pushed or pulled it along themselves," said Giselle. "It cut grooves in the ground and turned the soil over for planting. After the soil was plowed, the lumps had to be broken up and smoothed out with other equipment."

"Come on," said Dominique, tugging at James' arm. "Let's go inside."

"Maybe Brother Twelve's followers used that in the fields," said Sarah as James and Dominique disappeared into the shed. "I've been reading about him in a library book Uncle Steve gave me. Everybody worked here at Cedar-by-the-Sea, or on Valdes Island. They had huge gardens, an orchard, a dairy, greenhouses, chicken houses and a monstrous storehouse that they filled with thousands of jars of home preserves. The ordinary followers had to keep working until they had passed the 'test,' then the 'chosen' ones became true disciples and were taken to De Courcy. If they measured up. If they didn't, they could be separated from their families, demoted, sent from De Courcy back to Valdes, or from Valdes back to Cedar-by-the-Sea."

"I guess Brother Twelve decided who measured up and who didn't."

"Right. There was one woman named Georgia who worked in the fields from two o'clock in the morning until ten o'clock at night. When she fell down, the others swore at her and called her lazy and made her work in the warehouse sorting and stacking huge sacks of potatoes. When she was looking after the goats and following them all over the rocky hills, she fell and hurt her knee. They wouldn't let her rest or get first aid. They made her paint a shed teetering on the edge of a cliff, too."

"I can't understand why she wouldn't just leave," said Giselle.

"She was more or less a prisoner. The only way off the island was by boat. Besides, these people joined because they needed to believe in someone or something. They were controlled by fear — fear of being different, fear of being an outcast, fear of having nothing to believe in.

"Don't forget, Brother Twelve was a magician. People really believed he had supernatural powers. Not to mention that he used threats: of isolation, of banishment to Ruxton Island without food or water, of soul murder."

"Did you ask your uncle about articles on cults?" Giselle grunted as she reached for a cluster of berries.

"Yeah, he has a file he said I could borrow. If he can find it."

Just then James and Dominique came racing out of the shed, both talking at once. "We found a clue! It's a box. We can't reach it. Come and see!"

*"Viennent! Dépêchez-vous!"* Dominique was jumping up and down.

"We can't come right now." Sarah was half standing and half leaning on the ladder, which was leaning on a thicket of brambles.

*"C'est gros comme ça."* Dominique drew an outline in the air with her hands.

"We'll look as soon as we finish here, OK?"

When the four-litre plastic pail was full, Sarah and Giselle carried the ladder back inside.

James picked up a small mirror and pointed to the wall where a triangular piece of plywood had been nailed between two two-by-fours near the old workbench. "Can you see that slanty board up there?" He drew a diagonal stroke in the air with his hand. "There's a box behind it."

"I can't see anything," said Sarah.

"You have to look in the mirror." James shoved it toward her. "Stand in front of the wall and hold it up like this." He demonstrated.

"I think you're imagining things."

"Tilt it. Tilt the mirror," said Dominique.

Sarah stood for several seconds tilting the mirror this way and that. "Wait a minute, there *is* something behind there. Take a look, Giselle."

Giselle tilted both her head and the mirror. "I see it now," she said. "So how do you propose we get it out of there? It would take forever to move all this stuff out of the way." She gestured impatiently at the pile.

Dominique said, "*L'echelle!* The ladder! Lean the ladder over."

Getting the ladder into position was a four-person job, especially since they were afraid to lean it against the wall in case it broke through the old boards.

"I'll go up," said Sarah.

"Aw, come on. We found it, so me or Dominique should go," said James.

"No, it's not safe. I'd feel horrible if you fell. I'd better go. My legs are longer, so I can step over the missing rungs."

James watched as Giselle and Dominique held the ladder steady. Sarah crawled cautiously upward.

"That's it. You're almost there," said James. "Lean over to the right, Sarah, just a little bit. Keep going. Stop. Look down."

Sarah looked and saw the plywood, but she couldn't get her head close enough to the wall to see what was behind it. She reached down. "Oooh," she said and shuddered as her hand pushed through cobwebs. She felt the top edge of the box. "I can feel it, but I don't think I can get it out," she grunted. "I'll have to let go of the ladder and use both hands. Wait a minute. I feel a rope. It might be a handle." Sarah clutched the ladder with her right arm and pulled the box out of its hiding place with the other.

"There's something in it that rattles," said Giselle.

"I don't think I can hold it and get down. I'd better toss it." Sarah was only about two-and-a-half metres above the floor, but she had to negotiate seven steps and two gaps before she would be safe on the ground.

Sarah leaned against the ladder and it shifted a bit. She reached out and put one hand against the wall.

"Drop it," said James.

"*Oui. Laisse la tomber.*" Dominique raised her hands in the air.

"Maybe you two could hold that old horse blanket as a kind of net while I hold the ladder?" Giselle pointed with her chin.

They spread the blanket open and held it near the ladder and Sarah tossed the box. It landed safely and bounced a couple of times.

When Sarah had both feet on the floor, Giselle set the box on a small clear space near the edge of the workbench. The box was made of cedar and was only slightly bigger than her hand. It was thick with dust and spiderwebs. The brass screws that held the lid in place had been undone on three sides.

Giselle found a screwdriver and pried the lid gently. She looked inside. "Ah, *simonac*. Take a look," she said to Sarah.

"Let me see, let me see!" James and Dominique tugged at Sarah's shirt.

James' eyes widened. "Bullets!"

Dominique squealed as she peered into the box.

"We'd better show this to your dad," said Sarah.

Sarah and Giselle carried the full blackberry pail and James and Dominique carried the box up to the house.

"You'll never guess what we found!" yelled James, bursting through the door.

Uncle Steve looked into the box. He tilted it and the bullets rolled out into his hand. There were five brass cartridges, two centimetres long.

"We'll take them to the police station and find out what kind of a gun they're for. That box has been in the shed for a long time by the look of it. I wish I knew who put it there."

⬿

They parked at the rear of the Nanaimo RCMP station and went into the building.

"I think we can help you. Constable Samorin is a gun buff," said the receptionist. "I'll see if he's in his office."

The constable was in and he didn't disappoint them. "These could be for a Colt .32 or a gun about that size," he said thoughtfully. "About a four-inch cylinder."

"Could they be seventy years old?" asked Uncle Steve.

He nodded. "It's possible. Where did you get them?"

James and Dominique both started talking at once but when the constable heard the name Brother Twelve, he raised his hand. "Hold it a minute. You mean these may have been left behind by Brother Twelve?"

"We bought the house that people say belonged to him and the kids have been looking for traces of the colony. They found the box in a shed out back. Do you think bullets would have been packed in a box like this around the late 1920s?" asked Sarah's uncle.

Constable Samorin shook his head. "It's highly unlikely, but the museum might be able to help you with that."

They thanked Constable Samorin and headed for the museum.

"I'd suggest you leave it here and I'll have the curator take a look," said the young women at the front desk. She wore a badge that said VOLUNTEER. "He'll know where to look for information that might identify it. He'll give you a call if he comes up with anything."

# SEVEN

SEVEN

S arah and Giselle decided to make blackberry pies on Friday morning. They sat on the Baxters' porch in the shade while the pies were baking. Giselle had been doing more reading, as had Sarah, so they needed to compare notes.

"So what happened after Madame Zee and her husband moved here?" asked Sarah.

"Brother Twelve spent a lot of time with Mabel, that was her real name, and they got to be more than just friends. Brother Twelve's so-called 'wife' Elma was grief-stricken and went to Vancouver. Roger Painter was very jealous. He attacked Mabel in her tent, left her beaten and bleeding, and then left the colony in a rage. Mabel and Brother Twelve moved in together. She was very good at getting her own way, so she was determined to help Brother Twelve gain more money and power.

"She had a bad temper and took it out on the workers. She beat the horses, too, but when people complained to Brother Twelve, he said she was his eyes and ears and mouth, and that her orders were his orders."

"We should check the pies now," said Sarah, jumping to her feet.

Giselle looked crestfallen when she opened the oven. "Darn! The juice has bubbled over the top crust. I should have mixed more instant tapioca with the sugar to thicken it."

"Don't worry, Giselle. They'll taste just the same and it didn't bubble over into the oven, so it won't a mess to clean up." Sarah lifted the two pies out and set them on a cutting board, then took out a fork and dipped it in the juice. "Taste," she held it out to Giselle.

"Mmm. It *is* good." Giselle smacked her lips and put her arm around Sarah's waist. "We're good cooks. I'll come and get it later. It's too hot to carry right now."

"I looked up that info about the guns and ammunition they had on De Courcy," Uncle Steve said at lunch, between mouthfuls of pie.

"Did it mention a Colt .32?"

Her uncle shook his head. "They had heavy-duty guns, six rifles and a thousand rounds of ammunition. The disciples took turns guarding the forts, and I guess the women weren't permitted to handle guns, so they walked from one fort to another looking out for suspicious government boats."

Sarah told James and her uncle what she had read about the two women Mr. Otis had mentioned — Mary and Leona.

"Mary Connolly gave thousands of dollars to the Foundation. She had always been rich, but when she ran out of money, she was sent to Valdes and forced to scrub floors, wash windows, paint, dig the garden, chop wood, things like that.

"She was eventually sent back to De Courcy Island and supervised by Leona, who had been separated from her husband and threatened with banishment and soul murder if she didn't make Mary do exactly as she was told."

Sarah wiped the back of her clammy neck, leaned back in her chair and tried to relax. "Mary and Leona were isolated — the others were forbidden to speak to them. They lived in a warehouse with dirt floors and slept on straw mattresses. Eventually they were sent back here to Cedar-by-the-Sea where they worked seven days a week plowing and planting a garden that would provide 'food for the destitute.'"

"Plowing? Maybe they used the plow that's beside the old shed," James exclaimed.

"Could be," said Sarah.

"I'd better go check it with my magnifying glass." James carried his plate to the dishwasher and charged out the back door.

"I did find that file about cults and brainwashing, if you're interested, Sarah," said Uncle Steve. "I put it on the sideboard in the living room. I gathered the information when I was doing an article about Jonestown. Have you heard of it?"

Sarah shook her head.

"Well, it is one of the most famous examples of a modern-day cult."

"What happened?"

"A man called Jim Jones founded a church in the States called The People's Temple. His intentions were good — he wanted to create a paradise on Earth where all people were equal, wealth was shared and there was no private property." He paused to scratch his jaw. "He pretended he had supernatural healing powers, but it was all staged. Some of his trusted disciples helped him fake the 'healings.' He gained thousands of followers and soon became both powerful and wealthy. Nine hundred of his followers went to Guyana to establish the colony headquarters there in South America. Remind you of anybody?" He raised his eyebrows.

"Scary." Sarah leaned forward. "Did they actually think it was paradise?"

"No. They told their fellow followers in the States that it was, but they worked twelve hours a day in boiling temperatures, attended endless evening services and were publicly flogged if they disobeyed."

"Ugh. That's horrible," Sarah shuddered.

"When relatives of those in the commune started to get worried, seven American Congressmen and twelve others went in by plane to check it out ... Everything seemed fine — they were shown around and treated well — but as the guests were leaving, Jones' followers opened fire and five people were killed. The other fourteen escaped into the jungle, though ten of them were wounded, and managed to get to an airstrip and fly out. But the story has a heartbreaking ending. When the Guyanese army arrived at the commune the next day, they found more than nine hundred dead bodies."

Sarah gasped. "How did they die?"

"Poison. It was in their drink. Most people drank it willingly and even gave it to their children, although some had to be prodded. Jim Jones died of a gunshot wound, but nobody knows whether he did it himself or had one of his followers shoot him. The ritual was called White Night. They had rehearsed the whole thing."

Sarah laced her fingers together and stared at the floor as she imagined the scene — she suddenly felt sick.

"So this Jim Jones and Brother Twelve were a lot alike." Sarah held up her fingers one after another as she spoke. "They both got people to hand over their money. They both started colonies away from civilization, where they couldn't be watched. They both treated their followers cruelly and forced them to work."

"But Brother Twelve's followers were rich," said her uncle. "Or at least they were until he robbed them blind, while Jim Jones' people were nearly all poor. There were thousands of them, though, and they gave him whatever they had."

"What I still don't understand," Sarah paused, "is why his followers let him get away with it."

"I guess anybody can be vulnerable to the lure of a cult, given the right circumstances. One of the biggest attractions is the need to belong to a group with similar interests. Cults are seductive and can be very dangerous."

Sarah didn't say anything for several seconds, thinking about the horrors at Jonestown.

"Sarah, are you all right?" Her uncle's voice seemed to be coming from a great distance.

She jerked to attention and sucked in a deep breath. "Yes. I just can't get my head around it. I need something to *do*."

"Do you feel like raking leaves?"

"Sure."

James helped with the raking, too, and by four o'clock they had three big piles of leaves on the lawn.

"Let's jump in them, now," said James.

Sarah had not jumped in leaves since she was a kid, but what the heck. In the middle of it all, Giselle came to get her pie. For a few minutes Brother Twelve, Jim Jones and the unsolved mysteries seemed a long way away.

At nine o'clock that evening Uncle Steve knocked on the door. "There's a phone call for you."

"How are you doing, Hon?" Her mother's voice sound anxious when Sarah picked up the receiver.

"I'm fine, Mom. It's great here. The beach is perfect and the swimming's good and I met this girl named Giselle who lives next door. She and her sister, Dominique, speak French."

"I was starting to get a bit worried when I hadn't heard from you. I thought you might be having a hard time with James."

"No. He's not so bad. You won't believe what we've found out. Have you ever heard of Brother Twelve?"

"I know a bit about him. He's sort of a local legend."

"Well, he lived in Uncle Steve's house and we found the place in the woods where we think he built his House of Mystery. We're building a fort there, Giselle and Dominique and James and me. It's fun, but it's kind of spooky, too."

"Well, just be careful. Don't you go wandering around in those woods by yourself. There have been cougar sightings."

"Mom, honestly, I'm fine. Don't worry. It's fun looking for clues. Tomorrow we're going to De Courcy Island in the neighbours' sailboat to look for old buildings and stuff."

"You're going with adults I hope. Good sailors?"

"I'm sure the Tremblay's are safe. Anyway, how's Dad?"

"Fine. He's downstairs building another birdhouse."

"Great! That should make about ten of them now. Say 'hi' from me. I'll call in a few days."

"OK. Enjoy yourself."

Sarah had been worried that she wouldn't be able to

sleep for thinking about Jonestown, but her mother's call had changed that. She slept through the night without a qualm.

# EIGHT

EIGHT

They were scheduled to leave for De Courcy at ten and take a picnic lunch, so Sarah spent the first part of the morning packing sandwiches, mixing juice, filling water bottles and gathering necessities — towels, a change of clothes, swim suits.

All the while James chattered excitedly about going to De Courcy in the same kind of boat that Brother Twelve used to transport slaves. He was sure he was going to find buried gold.

This was the first time Sarah had been aboard a sailboat, so she was excited but also a bit nervous. She had seen them racing along the coast, leaning over so far the sails skimmed the water while everybody on board clung to the gunwales to keep them from capsizing.

There was a stiff breeze today, perfect sailing weather, according to Marc. He helped them aboard, distributed life jackets, pulled anchor and they were away! The masts remained comfortingly perpendicular, and it was exhilarating to be whisked along in a quiet world of wind and water. The only sounds were those of the sails snapping in the wind, the cries of the seagulls and the swoosh of the ocean in their wake.

The islands slowly grew larger and soon Marc yelled, "We're going to come about!"

*Come about? Come where, and about what?* wondered Sarah. She watched as Marc, looking like he was manipulating marionettes, pulled and slackened several ropes. Everyone ducked as the boom swung to the other side and almost instantly they were facing in the opposite direction. In a few seconds the boat was bobbing slowly on the waves and Marc was lowering the anchor.

De Courcy Island looked just as beautiful up close as it had from a distance. No wonder Brother Twelve's followers thought it was paradise.

Boats of all shapes and sizes were at anchor in the bay and on the shore dozens of families were setting up tents, cooking over campfires, building sandcastles, paddling kayaks, swimming, throwing Frisbees or playing beach volleyball. The air was full of laughing voices and summer smoke — campfires, barbecues, citronella candles.

Sarah tried to imagine the same scene seventy years earlier. People had lived here, but had they been allowed to relax or were they forced to work long hours of backbreaking labour before listening to the Master of Wisdom preach? Had he chastised them for not being obedient? There couldn't have been much time for fun and games if he was always watching them.

"This is a marine park, so you must not take anything from the beaches," warned Mrs. Tremblay. "*Il ne faut pas faire ça.*"

"Can we swim? Can we? *S'il vous plaît.* Please, please," begged Dominique.

Her mother nodded. "*Oui, ma chouchoute,* as long as you wear your life jacket and stay close to shore. Come, I'll help you. *Allez! Dépêchez-vous.*"

The water at Cedar-by-the-Sea was warm and relaxing, but here it was much colder. Sarah, Giselle, James and Dominique jumped off the dock and swam around in ever-widening circles. Mrs. Tremblay and James' father stayed on shore to keep an eye on the swimmers, but Marc dove in and swam parallel to the shoreline.

Sarah was still excited from the thrill of the sail. The invigorating water made her skin tingle. She felt giddy. She could sail a boat around the world. She could live on a mountaintop and study the remnants of an ancient civilization. There was nothing she couldn't do.

Mrs. Tremblay didn't want to swim, but Uncle Steve had his turn when the others were exhausted. When Marc came back from exploring, they had lunch on shore at a shady picnic table.

"I think I spotted the place where Brother Twelve might have had one of his buildings," said Marc. "About half a kilometre up shore." He pointed.

"Can we go?" asked Giselle.

"I think it would be too dangerous to try to land in the dinghy," he said. "But we could probably walk it. The tide won't come in for a few hours."

"Apparently," said Uncle Steve, "there was gold buried all over De Courcy, under barns and chicken houses, even under the schoolhouse. I brought the library book along and there are some maps and pictures that might give you a few clues," said Uncle Steve as he flipped through the book. He handed it to Marc.

While they were eating Marc managed to devour three sandwiches and study the maps at the same time. When he was finished, Marc left the library book with Uncle Steve and he and Sarah and Giselle got ready to leave on their search for remains of Brother Twelve's colony. James begged to go, but his father convinced him he should stay and mind the fort with Dominique.

Getting around and over the obstacles on the beach was a little, but not much, easier than getting through the undergrowth at Cedar-by-the-Sea. Driftwood logs were piled helter-skelter. Sharp promontories of rock blocked their path. Oyster beds and slippery, algae-covered sandstone made crossing tricky. There was little conversation because they were all watching where they were going. Finally Marc stopped and pointed up a low cliff. "I think the old building is right about there."

They could see a NO TRESPASSING sign and the remains of a barbed wire fence, so Giselle said she would wait on the beach and act as lookout while Marc and Sarah climbed up to have a quick look around.

"I think this must have been the school," said Marc, reaching out a hand to help Sarah up the incline.

"I read about that this morning before we left," said Sarah. "Wow!" She stopped dead in her tracks. The large building was made of wide, vertical cedar boards with narrow strips of wood covering the joins. Cedar shingles covered the roof. There was a small lean-to beside the front door. Framed dormers extended from the sloping roof to shade five windows. The wood was weathered and unpainted and tall, dry yellow grasses blurred the foundation. A thick stand of firs stood behind it.

Maybe it had been here for seventy years, empty, waiting for the sounds of scraping desks and chattering children. Sarah imagined that she heard whispered conversations, furtive grating and the echoes of a concrete block being lifted, boxes of gold coins being hidden and removed. If only she could go in!

A strange mixture of smells emanated from the building: a sweet scent like licorice mingled with the dry, sulphur smell of aging wood.

"It's all locked up," said Marc, trying the door handle.

She hurried to where he was standing, hoping to peek in a window.

"Spooky, isn't it?" she said, as she scrambled up on a log buried in weeds and grass and reached for the window frame nearest her. Suddenly something grabbed her ankle. She fell headlong into a patch of wild broom and vines and before she could recover, she thought she heard laughter, wild and taunting. She thrashed around, trying to free herself and get to her feet.

"Ah, *simonac*! Are you OK?" asked Marc, helping her up. "Your leg is bleeding."

"Just a scratch," said Sarah. She was trembling and her voice was shaking. "Did you hear something?"

"You mean the raven up there?" He pointed to the roof.

"I guess so," she said, but she didn't think it had been the raven. It had been a human voice, she was sure, but she didn't dare say so. *Who* or *what* had tripped her?

"You look pale," said Marc. "Are you sure you're all right? Maybe you sprained it?"

Sarah shook her head. "I'm fine. Really." She tried to make her voice sound normal.

"OK, if you're sure, we might as well look around while we're here. There must have been paths leading to some of the other buildings."

"I think I'll see if Giselle wants to change places with me." She hurried to the bank and called down for Giselle to come up.

Giselle did want to explore, but she wanted Sarah to stay, too. "I didn't see a single soul down there," she said.

The scratches on Sarah's leg stung, her skin was crawling and she was sure ghosts were lurking behind every tree, but Marc and Giselle were already several steps ahead, talking excitedly about the old school. Heat waves shimmered and distorted the landscape. She felt dizzy.

Marc stopped. "Look," he called. "See this?" He was standing on a small hillock, pointing down.

"What is it?" Sarah caught up to them.

"I bet there was gold buried here. See how uneven the ground is?" He grabbed a stick and gouged it.

A loud crack made Sarah jump. "What was that?" she whispered.

"A dry tree branch snapping. It's from the heat," said Marc.

"It sounded like a gun," said Sarah.

"It's just your imagination," said Giselle comfortingly.

Marc walked ahead and Giselle lingered beside Sarah.

"You go with Marc," Sarah said. "I feel like taking my time. I might even sit down for while."

"What's the matter?" Giselle put her arm around Sarah's waist.

"Nothing. I just scratched my leg a bit. You go."

Sarah's fall had bruised her ankle, but she was determined to pull herself together.

Marc and Giselle disappeared.

Suddenly Sarah heard a loud rustle in the bushes behind her. She clapped her hand over her mouth.

A small bird flew out of a thicket. Could a creature that small have made all that noise?

Marc came out of the bushes a few seconds later, his face beaming. "Come and see! We found an old building."

The building was practically falling down and there were no doors or windows. In a flash Sarah remembered Giselle's description of the forts. She pictured people climbing a ladder and disappearing through a trapdoor into a stash of guns and ammunition.

"I wish we could get in there, but there's no way of getting up on the roof," said Marc.

"Let's look around the other side," said Giselle.

"I'll wait here," said Sarah. She was sitting on a smooth rock, rubbing her ankle, when she noticed a wide crack near the base of the building. She knelt, shaded her eyes and peered into the interior. Light slanted down through a hole in the roof and she saw a door hanging by its hinges from the ceiling. So there *had* been a trapdoor there. As her eyes grew accustomed to the shadows she could see shelves and boxes covered with pine needles, leaves and dust.

"We didn't find anything," said Giselle, coming around the corner of the building.

"This was a fort all right. Look." Sarah stood and Giselle took her place.

After Marc took a look, it was time to go. They were back at the clifftop before Sarah had time to think about her ankle.

"I'll go first so I can help you if you have any problems on the way down," said Marc.

Sarah climbed down like a pro. She grabbed roots and shrubs to steady herself as she went, but she did *not* grab Marc.

Back at the beach she took off her shoes and washed the blood and grime off her leg with seawater. It really stung, so she was glad that Marc and Giselle were busy talking and didn't notice that her hands were shaking.

As they made their way back to the picnic site, she tried to distract herself with the sound of the lapping ocean waves and the reassuring smells of seaweed and saltspray. She convinced herself it had been a raven she'd heard, an ordinary vine that had tripped her, a snapping tree branch that had caused the loud noise and a bird that had rustled in the bushes.

Uncle Steve was sitting at a picnic table reading and Mrs. Tremblay, James and Dominique were on the beach hunched over a tidal pool.

Sarah sighed as she sank gratefully onto the bench.

"So tell me all about it. Did you find anything?" asked Uncle Steve, peering over the top of his glasses.

"We did!" said Marc. "We saw the old school and a building that must have been one of the forts. I wish I could have gotten inside, but it had no windows or doors and the trapdoor in the roof was too high."

Giselle jumped in. "Sarah found a crack in the wall and we saw boxes and crates inside!"

"Are you all right, Sarah? You look pretty pale," said her uncle.

"Fine. Just tired." She crossed her arms on the picnic table and laid her head down.

"I've just been reading about Brother Twelve. Listen to this." Uncle Steve opened the library book and paused to flip to a page where a dry stalk of grass served as a bookmark.

"Despite the fact that we know Brother Twelve was cruel and abused his followers, physically and emotionally, some women still fell under his spell. One woman said he was stimulating and wise and always spoke carefully and with sensitivity ... This is a direct quote, 'You felt his presence. He was carrying a lot of voltage.'"

"I don't understand how women could fall for him," said Giselle. "Look at that picture of him on the cover. Does he look handsome to you, Sarah?"

Sarah sat up. "No, but there's something about his eyes." She saw Marc looking at her with the trace of a smile and flushed.

Uncle Steve closed the book and tapped the cover with his forefinger. "You know, there's an account in here about how he met a married woman on a train between Seattle and Chicago, convinced her they had been lovers a thousand years before, in Egypt, and that their destiny was to have a son who would be the reincarnation of the god Horus. The son would become a world saviour. Believe it or not, she fell for it, hook, line and sinker. She left her husband, gave Brother Twelve twenty-five thousand dollars and he hid her in a cabin on Valdes Island away from the rest of the colony."

*"Maudit!"* said Marc. "That sure sounds like a crock. People really believed it?"

"They did. And Brother Twelve was already married, or at least living with a woman he *called* his wife."

"Did they have a child?" asked Giselle.

Uncle Steve shook his head. "No, they didn't. When things didn't work out the way he planned, Brother Twelve disowned her and left her alone and destitute on the island. She had a mental breakdown and ended her days in an asylum."

"Horus was the Egyptian god of the sun and he had the head of a hawk," said Giselle. "The sun god was special because he could fly across the sky with great speed."

# NINE

U ncle Steve was a speed-reader; he could scan printed material and get the gist of it three or four times more quickly than most people, so by bedtime that night he had practically memorized Brother Twelve's story.

"Giselle told me that Brother Twelve claimed he could murder souls." Sarah reclined on the couch, laced her fingers together and cradled her head, elbows out to the side. "Does the book say anything about that?"

Uncle Steve nodded, flipped to the index, then back to the text. "Here we are. Roger Painter had been one of Brother Twelve's most faithful disciples. During the court case he presented a letter he had received from Brother Twelve about that very thing — about how he 'killed' certain people who had thwarted his plans. This is what he said about it: Brother Twelve arranged his followers in a circle or triangle. He then chose someone he wanted to punish, imagined that person was standing in front of him and began cursing and damning their spirit. He cut the spiritual body from the physical body with hand movements — a vertical stroke going from the head downward, then a horizontal one from left to right. Supposedly, after this treatment, the body would waste away and eventually die."

"Did it work?" asked Sarah, afraid of the answer.

Uncle Steve shook his head. "There is no evidence that it did, although some did die later of pneumonia, 'intestinal stricture,' whatever that was, and strokes and heart attacks. The only death that was at all strange was a man who keeled over while preparing to make a speech about Brother Twelve."

"Do you think Brother Twelve really believed he could kill people?"

"It's hard to say, but all he needed to do was to convince his followers. And by the way, he did carry a Colt .32. Kept it in the inside pocket of his jacket. He put his hand on it when he was angry with somebody. That was near the end, when he got really paranoid."

Sarah was spooked. The story of the Jonestown tragedy came back to haunt her. She hoped she'd avoid nightmares, wild imaginings about being tripped and laughed at by ghosts, visitations from a monk in a brown robe and be able to sleep peacefully.

Before going to bed, she grabbed a broom and decided to sweep the ghosts out of every corner of the room — the dresser drawers, under the beds, inside the wardrobe.

Ginger sat outside on the porch and watched the flurry of activity with her ears cocked. The broom seemed to have taken on a life of its own, lunging under the beds, poking into the corners, scratching under the dresser, scurrying around inside the wardrobe. Mats were thrown out, shaken, taken in again. Drawers were yanked open, dusted and closed. All the while Sarah chanted, "Get out of my life. I don't believe in you."

The de-ghosting of the dresser drawers was easy, but just as Sarah was pushing the bottom drawer shut, something caught her eye: a narrow crack in one corner with something lodged in it. A dull, grey coat button? A lid from some kind of bottle? She tried to pry it out with her nail file. "Gently, gently," she muttered to herself. After a few tries the object popped out and landed with a clatter on the bare wood. It was a ring, or at least it was round. No telling what it was made of. Uncle Steve might know what it was; they must have brought the dresser with them when they moved in.

The house was silent except for the faint sounds of the news on the radio upstairs in her uncle's bedroom. The ring question would have to wait until morning. She set it on the mantel and prepared for bed.

When she asked her uncle about the old dresser the next morning, he said, "No, we didn't bring it with us, it was here when we arrived. We thought we'd refinish it one day."

"Well, this was in it." Sarah handed him the ring.

"Odd. Too big for a finger ring and too small for a napkin ring. It looks like it's been engraved. Just a minute, I'll get some silver polish and the magnifying glass." He yanked open a drawer. "Where is it? James!" he called.

"What? I mean, pardon?" James said through the screen.

"Have you seen the magnifying glass?"

"I'm using it. To look for more clues," he said.

"Brother Twelve might have hidden something out here."

"I need it for a minute."

"OK, OK," said James. He opened the door and reluctantly handed it over.

There were faint traces of a design on the ring: a friendship knot surrounding initials.

"It might be 'S. F.,' or no, I think it's 'S. P.,'" said Uncle Steve.

Sarah's eyes widened. "Those are my initials. Sarah Prentiss."

"So they are," said her uncle. "Then I think you should have it. Perhaps you can find out who it belonged to. Here's hoping it brings you luck."

"Are you sure I should keep it? Maybe we should wait until Aunt Trish sees it."

"Finders, keepers," said her uncle. "Besides it was *made* for you."

Three hours later the fort-builders were back at work. By two-thirty they had finished stacking ferns on the roof and leaning sticks and branches against the sides. Now they were getting to the interesting stuff. Giselle brought felt markers and sketches from an art book and James brought more driftwood, so he and Dominique started on the PRIVATE PROPERTY sign while the older girls worked on the Egyptian symbols for the doorway.

Giselle drew the outlines and Sarah coloured them in. First was a square cross with a looped top. Underneath it, Giselle drew what looked like a flat beetle, except that two wide antenna and four wide legs curved out from the body. Under that was a snake, sitting up on a skinny curled tail, one eye in its head. Rattles burst from its mouth. Then there was a side view of a sphinx with a lion's body and the head of a man. Its tail curled around a square base.

"That's one panel. We'll do other designs for the other side," said Giselle.

There was a line drawing of a chunky bird with short wings, its round head turned sideways to reveal a large eye and beak. Then a narrow bird, seen from the side, skinny legs, round head, round eye, skinny beak. Then two geometric designs — letters of the Egyptian alphabet? One looked a bit like a kite, the other was an upside-down "v" with a line curling into semicircles at both ends and intersecting the left downward stroke of the "v."

"What do these things mean?" asked Sarah.

"They're from ancient Egypt. At first when archeologists found symbols like this on the lids of coffins and places like that, they thought it was just for decoration, but then they found a way to decipher the language."

"How do you know so much about it?" asked Sarah.

"I had a history assignment at school last year."

"Listen!" Sarah held up her hand and cocked her head.

"What?" Giselle whispered.

Sarah gave her head a quick shake and strained into the wind. "Can you hear it?" she whispered.

Giselle shook her head. "Hear what?"

"A growling."

"Growling?" Giselle looked at her, puzzled.

"Yeah. Growling and hissing and squeaking, all at the same time. Shhh. Listen."

"I think it's just crickets or bees," said Giselle.

Sarah did not think it was crickets or bees. She was sure it was something a lot bigger than crickets or bees, but Giselle had turned back to the job at hand so Sarah let it go. Maybe she was getting paranoid, thinking she could hear through walls. Where was Ginger? Sarah called her and Ginger came running, her nose and front paws covered with dirt.

"She's been digging again," said James.

Sarah held her breath and listened. She could no longer hear the strange sound. "That looks great!" she called to Giselle, who had leaned the panels up against the fort entrance.

"Ours looks fabelluss, too," said Dominique. She and James set the sign on top of a stump covered with a piece of plastic daisy-patterned lace.

The spelling on the sign was close to perfect except for a missing "E" at the end of PRIVATE, and a double "E" instead of a "Y" at the end of PROPERTY. "Time to pack it in for today," said Giselle.

"Yeah. Do you think we should take the panels home just in case, you know, there's a bad storm or something?" asked Sarah.

"Good idea. Come on James, Dominique, let's get going."

"It's a holiday tomorrow and we're having a *cabane à sucre*. We'd like you to come," said Giselle as they were walking home.

"What is that, anyway?" asked Sarah.

"It's a party. It's lots of fun. You can help me with the *tourtières* and stuff."

Sarah lay in bed and breathed in the pungent smell of the sea as she gazed through the screen at the stars. She tried to think about the good things: the party the next day, the fort, the blackberries, the Egyptian hieroglyphics.

The silver ring, now hanging on a narrow leather cord, was under her pillow. When she looked at the engraving of the friendship knot and the initials inside it, she was sure it was meant for her. Perhaps it had been sent to her from someone she had never known. *It will be my talisman*, she thought as she drifted off to sleep.

"Sarah! Sarah! Come with me." A gentle voice awoke her, summoning. The man who stood at the foot of her bed was wearing a perfectly pressed soft grey suit, a white shirt and a tie, a felt hat with a curved brim and in his lapel, a red carnation. His eyes were full of love and tenderness. "Come, Sarah. Come with me to the boat," he said. "You will slip into the water. You will find your place with my Brothers."

"Yes," whispered Sarah.

The man moved noiselessly from her screened bedroom to the lawn, beckoning to her, his eyes pulling her toward him. "Come, Sarah. You will be my messenger from heaven."

In a few minutes they were at the water's edge and he was getting into a small boat. "Come, come with me."

"I'm coming." She was standing in ankle-deep water, making her way to the craft.

A woman's voice, faint and distant, was trying to enter her consciousness, but Sarah pushed it away. She must concentrate. She must follow.

The man in the grey suit looked back at her. His welcoming arms were open wide and his face wore a gentle smile.

The voice in her head grew louder. She stopped in her tracks. SHE MUST TURN BACK! She clenched her fists and gathered all of her strength. Her legs were too heavy to move. She would have to use every ounce of her will to resist.

Suddenly the man's shrieking voice rasped, "Do as you're told, silly fool!"

"No, no," she pleaded. She was paralyzed.

"Do as I say, wretch! Obey me or you will lose your soul!" he screeched.

She would not surrender. She backed up the beach and sat huddled on the sand, too weak to stand. His voice was gentle again. It surrounded her, coaxing her with its persuasive charm.

"Sarah, come. Don't be afraid. You must trust me. Come to the boat. You will join my Brothers in heaven and be my celestial guide."

She closed her eyes and clenched her fists. "No! No! Get out of my life! I don't believe in you," she sobbed.

Instantly all was quiet. Sarah's sobs subsided. She was lying on her back, staring at the sky. Ginger was licking her hand. She got shakily to her feet and stumbled up the beach to the house. Ginger kept pace with her slow footsteps and this time she followed Sarah into the room and settled herself on the mat by her bed.

Sarah brushed the sand from her body and cleaned a barnacle scratch on her thigh with water from her drinking bottle. She heard the man's terrifying cry and felt the pull of his gaze and yet surely it was a nightmare. She was sleepwalking again. Her reading must have planted the scene in her imagination. But what if it really *had* happened? What if she really *was* losing touch with reality?

# TEN

Sarah reached under her pillow and clasped the silver ring. There was a message for her there, she was sure. She had to learn more about Cedar-by-the-Sea. The more she knew, the more she would be able to resist.

"Snap out of it," she said aloud and pinched her arm. She closed her shutters, turned on the overhead light and flipped through the book for photos. There he was. This confirmed it: Brother Twelve's everyday attire was a grey suit, a fedora, a white shirt and tie, and a carnation in his buttonhole. When he went into the House of Mystery, though, he often wore a brown monk's robe. He had visited her in both guises. She was sure she had not known this before her nighttime encounters. Or had she?

She read on. The book described a typical visit to

the House of Mystery. Brother Twelve instructed his followers to stand silently outside the fence and wait for him. Hadn't she seen them that first evening? People saying, "Hush," looking frightened — that wasn't a dream. She had been wide awake. Hadn't she?

When Brother Twelve came out of the House, he trembled and writhed on the ground. He knew if anyone had spoken, and he knew what they had said, even though the fence was fifty metres away. He punished the rule-breakers, threatening to send them to Ruxton Island or murder their souls.

She read on. Brother Twelve had several mistresses — one or two actually lived in the House of Mystery — and others he visited when he said he was "fasting, meditating, or waiting for truths" to be revealed by his eleven Brothers. No wonder he built a fence and insisted that nobody go beyond it!

Sarah felt contempt, even revulsion for a man who cared so little for others that he terrified them only to profit from their labour. But, she had to admit, his story and presence were mesmerizing — his seductive voice, his piercing eyes, a hint of danger that was oddly attractive.

The Tremblay household was bustling when Sarah arrived the next morning for the *cabane à sucre*. Giselle's father and several other men unloaded picnic tables and wooden troughs from a truck. They carried blocks of maple sugar and big cans of maple syrup into the house. They assembled a platform on the edge of the yard. They set up barbecue grills and chopped kindling wood.

Mrs. Tremblay and another woman were unloading groceries from the car and checking off a list of supplies: ham, eggs, flour, drinks. They poured some of the maple syrup into smaller bottles and cut blocks of maple sugar into squares.

Sarah and Giselle raked the yard and strung coloured lights among the trees. They carried out tubs for ice and pop and tied garbage bags to the picnic table legs. The biggest job was making the *tourtières*.

"We need a hot oven — five-hundred degrees, OK?" Giselle brought out four pie plates lined with pie dough that she and her mother had made earlier.

"Will four be enough for everybody?" Sarah asked.

Giselle shook her head. "Other people are making them, too. This is my great-grandmother's recipe." She unfolded a piece of lined paper and flattened it on the countertop.

"We need a big pot."

Sarah opened a lower cupboard door and pulled out the biggest pot she could find.

"It takes one pound of ground beef or pork for each pie, so that's four pounds, and we mix it with onion, garlic, salt, savory, celery, ground cloves and half a cup of water." Giselle had started to open packages. "We have to chop up the celery and onions and make bread crumbs, but the crumbs don't go in until later."

After the meat mixture had simmered for twenty minutes, they stirred in two or three spoonfuls of breadcrumbs for each pie, then let it sit for ten minutes. Finally they poured the mixture into pie plates and added the top crusts.

"*Voilà!*" said Giselle as they finished trimming the extra dough around the edges.

"They're all ready for baking." They stood back and looked proudly at their handiwork.

Outside, the party was getting under way. Sarah had never seen anything like it. Voices chattered in both French and English, French songs played on the stereo, men set the wooden troughs beside the picnic tables and filled them with ice.

Giselle explained that if the *cabane à sucre* had been held in April, as was the custom, they'd have gone up the mountain to get snow, but there was no snow at Cedar-by-the-Sea, so ice would have to do.

Huge pots of maple syrup for the toffee sat on the stove in the kitchen and big casseroles were put into the oven to bake. Bacon and eggs and *crêpes Suzette* cooked while families sat at picnic tables eating, pouring maple syrup on every bite.

After the tables had been cleared they played baseball and held races. In the relay race each runner had to hold an orange under the chin and transfer it to a teammate without using any hands.

"Toffee's ready!" Soon the children were holding popsicle sticks and gathering around the troughs while pots of hot syrup were poured over the ice. They rolled the sticks around in the cooling goo and made maple toffee lollipops.

Dominique was yelling excitedly about *tire d'érable* and explaining to James that they had to hold a chunk of soft toffee between them and keep pulling it and folding it back on itself until it was creamy and smooth.

A horse and buggy rumbled up the driveway and the driver called loudly, "*Viennent pour une promenade!* Hayrides! *Allô!* Come for a hayride!" They crossed a farmer's field and rode along an old logging road where huckleberries grew, then back home by way of a horseback-riding trail through the bush.

A group of musicians from Port Alberni arrived and set up their instruments on the stage. They wore shirts with long puffed sleeves and coloured waist sashes with tassles that hung down to their knees, woolen toques to match.

Marc got home from work at the same time the band arrived.

"So what do you think?" He waved his arm at the crowd.

"Great," said Sarah. She wished she could think of something more interesting to say, but nothing came to mind, so she just smiled and nodded vigorously.

The band featured a violin, an accordion, a guitar and a singer. They played *"Au clair de la Lune," "Vive la Canadienne," "Un Canadien errant"* and *"Toujours tu seras mon amour."* The soloist sang one line and the adults sang the next, "— always you will be my love," then *"tes jolis yeux doux* — your lovely soft eyes."

Uncle Steve arrived in time for supper: ham, baked beans, *tourtières* and, for dessert, ice cream with maple sugar.

An orange harvest moon rose and the orchestra played on. People danced on the grass and in and out of the shadows. Mrs. Tremblay danced with James and Dominique, the three of them holding hands, and Giselle and Sarah danced together.

Marc leaned against a tree trunk with his arms crossed and tapped his foot in time to the music.

Early the next morning James came racing down the stairs waving a flyer. He wanted a new mountain bike.

"No way, unless you save half the money yourself," said his father.

"Half the *money*?" said James. "That will take forever."

"That's the way it is, son," said Uncle Steve firmly. "You can earn three dollars an hour raking leaves if you like."

The weather forecast seemed almost cheerful compared with James' mood: cloudy and dull with scattered showers, possibility of precipitation, sixty percent.

They had planned to go blackberry picking, but Giselle phoned and said Dominique was begging to go to the fort instead. James said "yes" for the first time since he got out of bed, so they were on their way.

James' outlook improved as they trekked into the woods, but the weather did not. The sky was heavy and grey and the forest seemed brooding. The tops of the trees were shrouded in mist.

As they approached the fort, Dominique screamed, "Somebody wrecked it! *Dommage!*"

Giselle, calm as always, was examining the damage. "I think it might have been a deer," she said soothingly. "It's OK, Dominique. We can fix it."

"How do you know it was a deer and not a bully?"

"Well, I'm not sure, but you see the way these branches are broken? They look to me like they've been trampled on by something four-footed, not a person." She stirred some broken twigs with the toe of her boot.

Sarah stood stock-still and looked around. It must have been a deer. What else could it have been?

They started to repair the fort, taking care to interlock the branches so they couldn't be knocked down so easily, but it was painstaking work and after twenty minutes Dominique begged James to play hide-and-seek with her. He was glad to take a break from the repair work. He had been training Ginger to "sit" and "stay" at home, but would she do it in the forest? Ginger sat with her ears cocked and when James called,

"Come" she raced to find them and retrieve her biscuit. Their voices sounded distant and muted.

Giselle and Sarah worked and picked up the story of Brother Twelve.

"I've been reading about cults," said Giselle, "and some of the things I've found out are pretty frightening. There are thousands of cults. Most aren't dangerous, but the bad ones can be deadly. No matter what the followers believe, they all end up serving the leader."

"So it's all about greed, power, control over other people, the leader getting his own way?" Sarah looked up.

"That's it. Actually it's hard to come up with a good definition because organizations like the army and fraternities can be *like* cults, you know, a group of people all working for the same thing. If their leaders aren't elected, they can abuse their authority and demand that their followers devote themselves as much to them as to the principles the cults uphold."

"So why do people join?" asked Sarah.

"Quite often the people who do are depressed, between relationships, jobs, traveling, moving to a new place, just divorced, that kind of thing."

"Uncle Steve gave me an article he wrote about brainwashing. I'm sure Brother Twelve did that."

"You mean there really is such a thing?" asked Giselle. "I thought maybe it was just an expression." She picked up a branch and started to poke it through a hole in the makeshift wall.

"It's real. The proper name for it is 'thought reform.' Often the person doing the brainwashing makes sure the odds are in his favour."

"What do you mean?"

"The leader doesn't reveal what the real goals of the organization are until it's too late, if ever. He also controls their schedule. People can still go to work, but they're told that when they're not working they must devote themselves to cult activities. After work, they put all their time into the organization."

"Yeah, I've heard of kids who turned their backs on their families and friends, even dropped out of school when they joined an organization like that. And then they hand over all their money," said Giselle with a flip of the hand.

"I know," said Sarah. "But you know sometimes I wish there was somebody who would just point me in the right direction when I get mixed up. I can see how the leader has more control if people feel powerless. The followers lose confidence so the leader tells them that that's normal and other people in the cult who have already been 'thought-reformed' believe it's normal, too."

"So instead of trusting your own common sense, you trust others," said Giselle.

"Yeah." Sarah chuckled. "I can't imagine *you* ever doing that, Giselle. You're so sensible. If I ever got lost, I'd like to be lost with you."

"Thanks." Giselle smiled. "I think."

"You have a mind of your own, but people in a cult *change* their minds so they aren't punished for disagreeing with the leader. They learn to take on the group's way of thinking and speaking. This usually includes a lot of jargon, so when group members talk to each other it shuts out those outside the group who don't know the language. If you learn well, you're rewarded; if you are slow or don't learn, you're threatened with shunning, banning, loss of privileges. Sometimes you're punished physically."

"We know Brother Twelve did that," said Giselle.

"He did. Nothing was done without his approval. There was no room for questioning or doubt."

"It's like they follow a formula," said Giselle.

"Exactly," said Sarah. "It *is* a formula and it's used

on prisoners of war and other ..." She stopped in mid sentence as Ginger bounded past.

Seconds later, James' panic-stricken voice yelled, "Help! Come quick! Sarah! Giselle!"

# ELEVEN

ELEVEN

It was hard to tell which direction the voice was coming from.

"Where are you?" yelled Sarah.

"Over here," called James, his voice scared.

Ginger followed the voice too and led them through the trees.

When Giselle and Sarah reached them, James was kneeling, peering over a ledge. "Dom-neek. Are you OK?" he yelled. "She fell down there," he pointed into the hole, as Giselle knelt beside him.

Giselle cupped her hands around her mouth. "Dominique, can you hear me? Quiet everybody. Listen!" she commanded. "Ginger, stay back!" she said angrily as the dog's front paws scraped the edge of the hole, sending a small cascade of dirt trickling down the sides.

"I can hear her," said James in a shaky voice.

"Shhh." Giselle grabbed his arm. "James, go over there by Sarah and keep the dog with you." She gave him a little shove.

Sarah put her arm around James and whispered, "Be very quiet and very still."

They watched Giselle as she lay down with her head turned sideways at the edge of the hole. "Are you all right, Dominique?"

"I think so," Dominique whispered as if from far away.

Sarah exhaled a breath of relief.

"It's all right. Don't move. We're here. We'll get you out, don't worry." Giselle's voice quavered on the last word and she sat up and looked around.

"We have to find out how deep the hole is," she said. "James, Sarah, run back to the fort and bring a long stick and the tape measure."

They took Ginger with them and were back in minutes.

Giselle was leaning over talking to Dominique in a quiet voice. She lifted her head. "She sounds all right."

"How will we get her out?" asked James.

Giselle called into the hole. "I'm going to poke a stick down to find out how deep the hole is, OK?"

They heard a small voice say, "OK," and then the shuffling of feet.

Giselle lowered the stick into the hole, scratched a mark on it where it was level with the ground and pulled it up. "Doesn't look too bad," she said as she laid it down.

Giselle held the tape measure case while Sarah pulled the tape out and they measured the stick. The hole was just less than four metres deep. Giselle pushed the button to retract the tape and handed it back to Sarah. "We'll have to be really careful that the sides don't collapse and cover her with dirt."

"It's all right," said Sarah. "We'll get her out. James, keep Ginger back from the edge."

Giselle had an idea. "We'll use the rope we used to make the fort!"

Sarah, James and Ginger thrashed their way through the undergrowth, gathered the rope and returned as quickly as they could.

They had six metres of rope altogether, but it was in two pieces.

"Tie them together," said Giselle. "James, you can help."

"Sure," said James. "I passed that test in Scouts."

James tied a square knot and Giselle and Sarah pulled it tight.

The rope didn't look too sturdy, but Giselle was sure it would be strong enough. It was the same size as the one they had used to tow the dinghy behind *The*

*Long Trick.* They made a loop in the end that could be loosened and tightened so that Dominique could slip it under her arms.

Giselle went back to the edge of the hole, walking around it and examining it from all angles. "This is the side we'll try," she said. "It looks like there are bits of concrete in the dirt wall."

They wrapped the end of the rope around a nearby tree trunk, then the three of them stood one behind the other with Giselle in front, all hands on the rope.

"OK, Dominique, the rope is coming down. You open the loop, pull it over your head and put it under your arms. Then hang on with both hands and climb up the side the rope is on. Put your feet against the sides like you're mountain climbing. OK?"

Sarah heard a faint "OK," then the words, "Over ... under ... hang on ... climb."

"Here we go," said Giselle.

They pulled and the rope tightened, but it didn't give. Then it moved several inches and they quickly took up the slack in a hand-over-hand motion.

Finally, a tousled red head and a smudged face appeared.

"Hurray!" they all yelled.

"Keep the rope tight," warned Giselle. She inched

forward with one hand on the rope and pulled Dominique up over the edge with the other.

Dominique was dirty and her knees were scraped, but she grinned at them and then everybody was talking and nobody was listening and they didn't even notice it had started to rain.

"How did you fall in the hole?" asked Giselle.

"I didn't think it was deep. *C'était petit comme ça,*" Dominique held her arms up to form a circle. "It only looked this deep." She held her hands five palm-widths apart. "It was big enough for me to hide in. But when I jumped down, I kept on going."

"Like *Alice in Wonderland,*" said James.

"*Oui.* Like that," said Dominique.

They were soaking wet by the time they got home, but nobody cared. They were so glad Dominique was fine that by the time they got to the Baxters' house and started to tell Uncle Steve what had happened, Dominique had *become* Alice in Wonderland. James interjected that he had tied the knot.

Uncle Steve was worried and said he would take a look and then fill the hole in with dirt. "We don't want this sort of thing happening again," he said.

Sarah and James put on rain gear and rubber boots, but Dominique stomped around the Baxters' kitchen, indignant that she and Giselle had to go home. It wasn't fair, she said. She should be helping, because after all, it was her hole, she had discovered it. Giselle insisted that their mother was expecting them and promised they would go back and look at the hole again the next day.

When the Baxters and Sarah had reached the spot for the second time that day, they shone a flashlight around the hole from every direction.

"This is part of a concrete foundation," Uncle Steve said. "There must have been a building here at one time. There are also some pieces of wood down there."

"Maybe it was the House of Mystery!" Sarah said excitedly.

"Maybe," said Uncle Steve.

"Maybe there was a trapdoor in the floor. Maybe he kept food and supplies in it."

"Possibly," said her uncle. "He claimed that he fasted when he was meditating, but he probably did keep a stash of food hidden away where nobody would find it. I'll have to get the hole filled in. If this story gets out, we'll have all kinds of snoops crawling around here."

"Yeah, but maybe there's something down there that would give us a clue."

"The rain's too heavy now. Tomorrow I'll bring a wheelbarrow and shovel and I'll go down and pick up anything I can find."

By two o'clock that afternoon the view out the huge front window had darkened. The islands were hidden behind a wall of grey fog and ships' whistles and foghorns moaned intermittently.

James was playing, so Sarah took the library book to her room. It didn't look any more cheerful than the weather, so she reached up and pulled the string hanging from the overhead light. Nothing happened. She tried again — still no light. She would have to ask Uncle Steve for a new bulb, but in the meantime she lit a candle, placed it on a small nightstand beside her bed and plumped up her pillows.

She decided she did *not* want to read the library book right now, so she pulled a crossword puzzle book and pencil from her pack.

After an hour, the rain had slowed to a fine drizzle so she thought she could go for a walk. James and Uncle Steve said they'd join her.

She wished that she could hate Brother Twelve, and she did in a way, but she couldn't help feeling a bit like all of those women who had fallen in love with him too — it was unsettling and more than a little bit confusing.

"The light in my room isn't working," Sarah said as they were getting ready to leave.

"I guess the bulb's gone. No problem." Uncle Steve got a light bulb out of the kitchen cupboard and walked to her room. When he reached up and pulled the string, the light went on.

"Hey, that's weird. I couldn't get it to work earlier," said Sarah.

"It seems fine now, but I'll leave the new bulb here in case you have any more problems."

As they headed down the beach, James said, "There's the old guy." A stooped figure in a yellow raincoat was bending to pick up pieces of bark and tossing them into a large galvanized pail with a wide spout at one side.

"What kind of a pail is that?" asked James. "It looks like it's a hundred years old."

"It's a coal scuttle," said his father. "And you're right, it probably *is* a hundred years old. Everybody used coal for heating and cooking in those days."

"Hi, Mr. Otis," yelled James.

The old man straightened up and tilted his head

to peer at them as they approached. "Who are you?" he asked.

"I'm James. Remember? I live right there," James pointed. "And this is my dad and my cousin."

"It is, is it? You sure you live there?" the old man barked. He looked at James suspiciously and plunked the coal scuttle down.

"Hello, Mr. Otis. I'm Steve Baxter. We bought the house next door," said James' father, offering his hand.

"And you and I met the other day. I came with Giselle. We brought cookies, remember?" said Sarah.

"Maybe I do and maybe I don't."

Sarah was wearing the ring she had found and it glinted as a beam of sunshine flitted between the clouds. Mr. Otis stared at the ring, then at her face, then back at the ring. His mouth dropped open.

"Heaven preserve us," he said with a scowl. He shook his head. "You're not Sarah."

He pointed at the ring. "Why are you wearing that ring around your neck? That doesn't belong to you."

"You mean you've seen it before?" asked Sarah. What if ...? Had Mr. Otis seen the ring when he was a child? She pulled the necklace over her head and handed it to him.

He studied it for a long time, nodding his head

and repeating her name over and over before giving it back to her.

"She used to wear it with a scarf," he said finally. "She looked so pretty when she wore it that way."

Of course! It was a scarf ring — too big for a finger ring, too small for a napkin ring.

She and her uncle exchanged a look. The blood was pounding in Sarah's temples and her skin prickled with goosebumps. She wanted to do two things immediately, if not sooner. She wanted to search through the index of the library book and look for references to someone whose first name was Sarah and she wanted to show Mr. Otis the leather handle they had found and ask him if he had ever seen it before.

Mr. Otis said goodbye and walked off so they continued along the beach.

"So that's a part of the mystery solved," said Uncle Steve. "We know what the ring was used for. Coincidence that the owner had the same first name as you do."

*Maybe it is, maybe it isn't,* thought Sarah. She was beginning to wonder if the strange things that were happening were happening for a reason.

The trees were blurry, their tops shrouded in mist. Anything could be out there, including a ghost ship called *The Lady Royal* on its way to Valdes Island.

# TWELVE

Uncle Steve kicked her out of the kitchen to make his famous stir-fry, so Sarah curled up on the chesterfield with the library book. Who was the Sarah Mr. Otis had talked about? Her last name must have begun with the letter "P" if the scarf ring belonged to her.

PUCKETT, SARAH! The name leaped off the page. And there were five references. She turned to the first.

Sarah Puckett, a spirited seventy-six-year-old retired schoolteacher from San Francisco, joined the group. Sarah flipped back the pages to find the year — there it was, 1930. Sarah Puckett had turned over her government pension to the Foundation and before long she was appointed to the advisory council. But Brother Twelve soon dissolved the council and as she was too old and lame to be useful to him, he ordered her to drown herself by falling backward out of a rowboat. Her spirit would return from death to report on the afterlife. She allowed herself to be rowed back and forth in deep waters, but in the end, her faith in God was stronger than her faith in the Aquarians and she refused to follow his orders. As a result, she was cursed and made an example.

Sarah's palms perspired and she breathed rapidly. It was just like her nightmares — the seductive voice coaxing her to the boat, the promise of an exalted place in heaven ... Brother Twelve still wanted something. But what was drawing him back from the dead?

There was something else she wanted to know about Sarah Puckett. What happened to her after Brother Twelve and Madame Zee escaped?

Although some of the followers had agreed to stay on at De Courcy after their leaders had abandoned them, many left. In September 1935, Sarah Puckett and another couple departed for Oceano, California. In a farewell note to friends, Sarah wrote: *We kept the faith. We did our duty. We finished our task. We have been released from "old obligations" and are now free to bid farewell.*

The words, written more than sixty-five years ago, were like poetry. Keep the faith. Do your duty. Finish the task. Many people would argue that Sarah Puckett had been duped because she believed that her time had been well spent even after she learned that Brother Twelve had ruthlessly used her money and her labour for his own gain.

Sarah fingered the scarf ring. It did have a message for her just as Mr. Otis must have left a message for Sarah Puckett with his sign. She took out her notebook and copied Sarah Puckett's parting words into it.

One evening a week James was allowed to use his father's computer, so while he and Uncle Steve were engrossed in what looked to Sarah like a very complicated cartoon puzzle, she walked along the beach hoping to see Mr. Otis. She could hardly wait to talk with him again.

He was sitting in his rocking chair on the porch, reading a book with large print.

He seemed more alert than usual and recognized her immediately.

"You told me that this was a scarf ring that used to belong to somebody you knew a long time ago," Sarah fingered the ring hanging around her neck. "Was her last name Puckett, by any chance?"

"That's it!" The old man beamed. "Sarah Puckett.

She was a kind woman. Never meant harm." He leaned back in his chair "She smelled nice — like lavender. She helped us with our work sometimes. Walked with a limp."

Walked with a limp! Sarah remembered the first night at Cedar-by-the-Sea. The creaking bed. The low moans. The limping footsteps.

"Mr. Otis, I found something else I'd like to show you, in case you might remember it. Could you take a look?

"Sure," he said.

"Look at this." She pulled the leather handle from her pocket and handed it to him.

He reached for it, then withdrew his hand. "Where did you get it?"

"We found it in the woods behind the house. That house over there, where James lives." She pointed.

The old man reached for the leather object again, examined it, then grasped it in his hand and made whipping motions. "Quirt," he said.

"What's a quirt?" asked Sarah.

"Haven't you ever ridden a horse?" said the old man.

"You mean it's a riding whip?"

"Yep."

"Could it have been from when Brother Twelve was here?" she asked.

"Madame Zee. She had a quirt and she knew how to use it."

"What do you mean?"

"The horses." A look of terror passed over the old man's face. "I never saw her use it on people, but I heard she did, sometimes."

"Madame Zee used a whip on *people*?" Sarah was shocked. She leaned closer to Mr. Otis. "Were you afraid of her?"

"Everybody was afraid of her."

Sarah forced herself to be calm. There was one more question she wanted to ask. "Do you think these things — the whip handle and the ring — could be part of some kind of black magic, or something? Say, to cast spells, or bring back ghosts?" She held her breath.

He frowned and said, "Can't say I believe in ghosts."

"But what would you do if they did? Have evil magic, that is?"

"Find something that has *more* magic, like they did in the court case," Mr. Otis argued.

"My uncle told me about that. That was amazing. People actually believed that a small stone could protect them from evil."

"Yep." Mr. Otis nodded, rose slowly to his feet and said, "Good night, young lady."

"Good night, Mr. Otis. Thanks," said Sarah.

As soon as she got back to the house Sarah went to tell her uncle another part of the mystery was solved. He and James were still upstairs sitting at the computer.

She tapped on the door. "It's from a quirt," she said matter-of-factly. "Mr. Otis is pretty sure." She handed him the leather handle. "Madame Zee used it."

"Really?" he said, taking the handle. "So it would have been attached to a braided rawhide lash." He held the leather handle in his right hand. "A picture of it and some information about it would make a good sidebar to my story."

"Do you think it could be the whip Brother Twelve used on the slave boat?" said James.

"Well, I guess it *could* be, but Mr. Otis said Madame Zee used it on the horses."

"Can I hold it?" James studied the leather handle. "What's a rawhide lash anyway, Dad?"

"Rawhide just means it was made out of rough leather, not smooth, tanned leather like you see now. The lash part would have been narrow lengths of this kind of leather braided together."

"Hey. That would sting!" said James, his eyes wide.

"You bet it would," replied his father.

"Poor horses." James looked sad.

"I'm going to phone Mom," said Sarah, heading for the stairs. She let the phone ring six times and was just about to hang up when she heard her mother's breathless voice.

"I was out in the garden," she said. "How are you getting along, Sarah?"

"OK I guess, but you wouldn't believe the things that have been happening. Dominique, she's Giselle's little sister, fell in a hole out near our fort. We got her out, but we're pretty sure the hole was a cellar under Brother Twelve's House of Mystery where he went to meditate."

"Well, you're having an interesting time by the sounds of it. You're sure you're all right?"

"Yeah. I feel weird sometimes — the stuff I've been finding out is scary, but ..."

Her mother interrupted. "Sarah, you don't have to stay. We'll make some other arrangement if you want to come home."

"No, no. I'm having fun. I want to stay. We went to a *cabane à sucre* at the neighbours' house and we went to De Courcy Island and saw some of the old buildings Brother Twelve built there. I found a scarf ring that belonged to a woman who was here with Brother Twelve. Mr. Otis next door told me."

"Well, it sounds like there's never a dull moment, but I'll be glad when you're home, Sweetie. We miss you."

"Miss you, too, Mom. Say 'hi' to Dad."

It was Wednesday and Mrs. Tremblay had invited Dominique and James to go to a play at the Chemainus Theatre in the afternoon, so Sarah and Giselle went to the fort by themselves.

The forest was green and fresh after the rain and the fort looked more settled, as though it had been there for a long time.

"It's so quiet here," said Sarah as Giselle adjusted the Egyptian panels. She stepped back, half-closed her eyes and studied the effect. "You know what I can't help thinking?"

"No."

"I can't help thinking about the slaves and servants who were sacrificed in the days of the Pharaohs. Paintings exactly like this were probably the very last things they saw before they were killed and sealed up in a pyramid to serve their master in the other world."

"Speaking of serving masters, I read about something that's really bothering me. It's about a girl our age." Sarah reached down and yanked up tufts of grass as she spoke.

"Does it involve Brother Twelve?"

Sarah nodded. "She was one of his followers," she said hesitantly.

"What happened?"

"This girl was only thirteen." Sarah kicked a shower of dirt over her shoe. "They took her away from her mother and sent her to Valdes Island. When she came back ..." Sarah drew in a ragged breath and spoke barely above a whisper, "her older sister said that she was all bruised and confused and didn't understand what had happened to her."

Giselle started pacing back and forth. "So I guess if that happened to one girl then it must have happened to others, too. Some people think they can do what-ever they want in the name of religion. *Dégoûtant!* Soul murders, being banished to Ruxton Island, all of it!"

"What if it's possible there really *are* ghosts here —Brother Twelve and others?" said Sarah.

Giselle shook her head. "*Non.* I don't believe in ghosts. He's not even alive anymore and when he was, he was just a fake, a bully, a selfish, greedy magician who fooled people into believing he was a saviour. Why, do you believe in ghosts?"

"No!" Sarah said emphatically, trying to convince herself. "Let's talk about something else."

Sarah was relieved to find her light worked when she was getting ready for bed. She slept through the night without any ghostly visitors.

"I'll clean up the breakfast dishes, Uncle Steve," she said when she finished her toast and cereal the next morning.

"Thanks, Sarah, I'd like to get that hole filled in this morning, before we get treasure-seekers here. When I went to the library I did some photocopying of old newspaper reports. After Brother Twelve and Madame Zee escaped by boat in the middle of the night, dozens of people went hunting for the gold. They ransacked and tore apart the colonists' cabins, dynamited the wells and dug all over the islands, but nobody found any gold. All the guns and ammunition disappeared, but that was probably the looters. We don't want that happening here."

"Yeah. When it comes to buried treasure, people will do almost anything," said Sarah.

"I read about a caretaker on De Courcy Island who kept bumping his head on the ceiling of a chicken coop because the floor was too high. He ripped it up and found a trap door. On it was a message in chalk that said, FOR FOOLS AND TRAITORS — NOTHING!"

"So Brother Twelve stole the money and then taunted those he stole it from!" said Sarah.

Her uncle nodded. "There was one man who lived on Gabriola Island who *did* benefit, though. He was not among Brother Twelve's followers, but he helped with the transporting of materials to the colony. He was given the remaining groceries — hundreds of pounds of sugar and flour and countless jars of preserved food. Some thought he helped with the escape, but that was never proven."

Uncle Steve went off with a wheelbarrow, a shovel and some rope and James persuaded Sarah to go out with him to have a *really* good look at the wooden skeleton of the old plow in the backyard. The handles were shiny and smooth and when Sarah grasped them, they felt warm to her touch, almost as though someone had just finished using it. She closed her eyes and tried to imagine Leona and Mary pushing it, but instead she saw them pulling it like a team of oxen.

"Dad's back." James said, racing toward the house.

Uncle Steve carried a cardboard box to the front porch and sat down to examine the contents. "I think the well was built into the floor of the building we think was the House of Mystery," he said, holding up some chunks of wood. He pulled out some smaller pieces of rough cedar and a short piece of sisal rope. "Look at this, would you? It's the same kind of wood that was used to make that box the bullets were in."

"Maybe this one was used for gold," said Sarah.

"It's possible, but it could have been used for foodstuffs or tobacco, too. There was no sign of gold at the bottom of the hole, that's for sure. There was broken glass, though." He gingerly lifted a chunk of glass from the box. "Look at this." He scratched his fingernail over the surface then rubbed the substance that he had scraped off between two fingers. "Wax. They poured wax over the gold coins."

"Like Mom does with jam jars," said James.

"Maybe he kept at least one box of gold under the House of Mystery in case he needed money in a hurry," Sarah said.

"Makes sense. The boxes were made for the jars of gold, but Brother Twelve kept his bullets in one of them." Uncle Steve gathered the wood and glass bits and put them back in the box. He stood, bent his elbows and rotated his shoulders. "Another piece of the puzzle solved."

# THIRTEEN

B y Friday afternoon, Sarah knew she had to go back to the fort, and she had to go alone.

The deer path felt different to her now as she walked through fallen leaves, flat and soggy. The sounds seemed louder, the smells more pungent, the twists and turns more numerous than she remembered. Leona and Mary must have worked the gardens close to this spot. She closed her eyes and tried to hear their voices. What would they say?

"*What if the master is a trickster. That can't be. How does he hear through walls? I've seen him with my own eyes, throwing fire from his bare hands. Shhh, he can hear us now. He'll punish us. What more can he do? Our rations are cut to the bone. I haven't seen my husband for weeks; he's not allowed to speak to me. The master can send us to Ruxton Island, or murder our souls and we'll spend eternity in hell. Shhh, shhh. Keep working.*"

Sarah walked to the chunk of concrete that Uncle Steve had pulled out of the hole. The mound of earth where the hole had been made it look like a grave. She wandered around the small clearing. A blur of purple under an old rose bush caught her attention. She knelt and picked a bouquet of Michaelmas daisies and placed them on the mound of earth. The words "Rest in Peace" kept repeating themselves in her brain.

"Brother Twelve," she whispered, "be gone." Her legs started to tremble and she felt weak. She sat down and buried her face in her arms. Suddenly she shuddered and her head jerked up. Somebody was staring at her — a blurry figure with a small, pointy beard and a thin angular face, two piercing light grey eyes. His arms were outstretched. She recognized him from the book and from her dreams.

"Sarah, come."

"Yes." Her eyes were wide and unblinking.

Her body felt light, as though she could float. She kept whispering, "No, no, no, no," as she slowly moved closer to the outstretched arms. She was almost there. She could reach out and touch his hand.

She stumbled and felt something solid and cool touch her chest. The scarf ring! She pulled it from under her T-shirt and clasped it tightly between her palms. She knew in her head that it did not have magic powers, but holding it might summon Sarah Puckett to her side.

She straightened her back and squared her shoulders. "Go!" she commanded loudly and slashed her hand up and down in front of the figure. Then twice more, "Go! Go!" The words echoed back and forth through the forest until every bush and tree seemed to be saying, "Go … go … go … go." The image of Brother Twelve dissolved.

Sarah sank gratefully to the ground with tears of relief in her eyes.

As the last faint echo of the word "go" faded into silence, she made herself a promise: she would try to control her own life and if she needed help or advice, she would make sure the person she asked was trustworthy — her parents or a good friend, someone like Giselle.

She headed back along the deer path.

When she got home her uncle said, "The museum curator phoned. The bullets were definitely made around the right time to have been used by Brother Twelve. The box is also quite old, judging by the type of screws that were used, but it was homemade, probably for some specific purpose. We'll never know for sure, but it's a good bet it was made for holding jars of gold coins."

They went over the clues they'd gathered so far.

"We've found a whip handle," said Sarah, "a scarf

ring, bullets in a box that was most likely made to hold gold and a hole in the ground. These things have been here all along, so why are we finding them now?"

"Coincidence, Sarah, and the fact that you're looking."

It was Saturday. Sarah would be going home tomorrow, and Dominique was finally going to have a chance to burn witches' hair in a campfire.

Sarah and James were the first to arrive at the beach in front of the Tremblays' house. The rim of a truck wheel had been moved onto the sand and a mound of dry twigs and driftwood was piled beside it. A big log that had been well tunneled by teredo worms faced the ocean and several folding chairs were stacked nearby.

James carried a plastic squirt gun and a walkie-talkie he had made from two empty soup cans and the wire he had found at the fort site.

Sarah settled on the log beside the fire pit. She could hear the sea and smell the sweet wild blackberries. She closed her eyes. She felt strange — light and heavy at the same time.

Mrs. Tremblay arrived carrying a cooler just as Uncle Steve approached with a bag in one hand and a camera in the other.

"My husband sends his apologies," she said. "He had hoped to be here, but there's a power outage some-where and he was called in to work." She started to arrange newspapers and twigs for the fire.

"Sarah, would you come and help me with these darn things, *s'il vous plaît?*" Giselle called, juggling several long hot dog forks and a folding stool.

James and Dominique crept around the driftwood, crouching down from time to time to mutter and then listen to the soup cans.

The buns were fresh, the hot dogs fat and juicy, the mustard tangy, the ketchup savoury, the marshmal-lows gooey, and for the next hour there was a lot of roasting and toasting and testing and tasting and chewing and swallowing.

Mrs. Tremblay played the guitar while the others packed up the leftovers. They sat around the campfire and sang songs, some English, some French, while the sun set.

"Would you like me to show you how Brother Twelve did some of his magic?" asked Uncle Steve, standing close to the fire. The gang nodded. He stood with his arms at his side, fists closed and chanted, "Come ye spirits, from the four corners of the earth." He turned in a slow, trancelike manner as he spoke. "Spirits of the world, come be with us." Suddenly he wheeled around to face the campfire, raised his arms, opened his palms and cried, "I now call fire down!" With a crackle and a hiss, a column of orange flame leaped from his hands.

"How did you do that?" asked James.

"Do it again," said Dominique.

"It's easy. I just dropped dry pine needles into the flames. That's what Brother Twelve did, too. He didn't drop them himself, but he had a trusted helper throw them at the right moment, so nobody would notice. That's not all. His disciples also put on blue robes and held a secret ceremony around a concrete altar painted with Zodiac symbols. One of the disciples threw a pail of water on a pile of leaves and twigs and it burst into flames. Brother Twelve had put white phosphorous in the pail along with the water, so the twigs caught fire."

Dominique, who had been poking at the sand with a stick, suddenly raised her head. "Marc!" she cried and raced to meet her brother.

"I thought you had to work late," said Mrs. Tremblay.

"It wasn't busy, so I got away early," said Marc.

He was carrying a faded folding canvas chair and he set it between Sarah and his mother.

"Have you eaten? Do you want a hot dog? There are

some left," said Mrs. Tremblay.

"Sure." Marc sat in the chair and wiggled it around with the weight of his body until it was solid on the sand. "Dad was telling me that he told some of the guys at work about us seeing the old schoolhouse on De Courcy and the caretaker said he knew how Brother Twelve could hear through walls. He had a microphone system — the assembly hall was bugged and there were wires from the House of Mystery to the fence, where the crowd waited for him to come out."

"The man was a first-class scoundrel," said Uncle Steve . "Do you know I was reading today that he even pretended to be a vegetarian because some of his followers were, when in fact he kept the best cuts of meat and other gourmet foods for himself. Meanwhile, people on De Courcy were on food rations — a slice of brown bread and a little jam each day."

"And he fed his dog chocolate," said Giselle, "but the people didn't get any."

"Remember how Ginger growled when we were building the fort, Giselle?" prompted Sarah.

"*Oui.*"

"And James found that wire? And Ginger was digging under a tree?"

"OK," said Giselle, nodding.

"The microphone system. I bet the wire James found was part of it and some of it's still there. When Ginger was growling, I could hear her even though she was far off."

"That means our fort must be between the House of Mystery and the fence," said Giselle.

"Well, that was long ago. Right now let's have more music," said Uncle Steve, so they had more songs while Marc ate two roasted hot dogs in one bun, followed by several toasted marshmallows browned to perfection by Giselle.

"Marc, tell us *The Long Trick* poem," said Dominique sleepily.

"Yeah, Marc. Tell us *The Long Trick* poem," said James.

Marc leaned back, laced his fingers behind his neck, and stared into the embers for a few seconds. When he spoke, his voice was clear and measured.

*I must go down to the seas again, to the lonely sea and the sky,*
*And all I ask is a tall ship and a star to steer her by,*
*And the wheel's kick and the wind's song and the white sail's*
*    shaking,*
*And a grey mist on the sea's face, and a grey dawn breaking.*

*I must go down to the seas again, for the call of the running tide*
*Is a wild call and a clear call that may not be denied;*

*And all I ask is a windy day with the white clouds flying,*
*And the flung spray and the blown spume, and the sea-gulls crying.*

*I must go down to the seas again, to the vagrant gypsy life,*
*To the gull's way and the whale's way where the wind's like a*
*whetted knife;*
*And all I ask is a merry yarn from a laughing fellow-rover,*
*And a quiet sleep and a sweet dream when the long trick's over.*

Marc's voice and the rhythm of the poem accompanied the pulse of the tide. "Sea Fever," he said. "Written in 1902 by John Masefield."

Sarah turned away and stared at the forest.

"Well, I think it's time we packed it in," said Uncle Steve.

They folded up the chairs, gathered up the picnic supplies and poured water on the fire.

"I'll walk partway with you," said Giselle, putting her arm around Sarah's waist.

"Thanks." Sarah felt tears sting her eyes and she quickly brushed them away with the back of her hand. The girls strolled along, arm in arm.

"Sheesh," said Sarah. "This sure didn't turn out the way I thought it would. I expected to be bored out of my tree with just James for company, but two weeks have gone by in a flash. I can't believe it."

"I know," said Giselle. "I'm so glad we met. It was fun building the fort. It was like a real-life scavenger hunt, finding out about Brother Twelve's colony."

"It *was* fun, but I'm glad that part of it's over. I kind of, you know, got scared sometimes — he seemed real to me, like I could see his ghost."

"Really?" said Giselle. "That must have been horrible."

Sarah nodded. "Yeah. It was scary. He seemed to be trying to get me to go with him," she gave a nervous laugh. "But of course, it was probably all my imagination."

"Are you still afraid?" asked Giselle anxiously.

"No! It's OK now, mostly because I had you to talk to. You know what Uncle Steve would say about you? He'd say that girl has a good head on her shoulders. And you do, Giselle. I'll miss you." Sarah sighed. "I guess I won't be seeing you much. We'll stay friends, though, won't we Giselle? Phone each other and visit when we get a chance?"

"For sure. You can come and stay with me anytime, my mom said so."

"Goodbye then," said Sarah, hugging Giselle.

"*J'espère que je te revoire bientôt!*" Giselle hugged her back.

They went their separate ways, stopping to wave at each other as the distance between them widened.

## ACKNOWLEDGEMENTS

I wish to thank Joy Gugeler, whose suggestions, enthusiasm, encouragement and meticulous editing have enlivened the process and contributed in large measure to the writing of this novel.

Thanks to John Oliphant for permission to quote from his book, *Brother Twelve*, and to Ross Tremblay and Carol Woodson for providing information about the French Canadian culture and language.

Marion Woodson is the author of *Mid's Summer: The Horse Race* (Pacific Educational, 1989), which was a Canadian Children's Book Centre Our Choice selection and was nominated for the Manitoba Readers' Choice Award. She is also the author of *The Amazon Influence* (Orca, 1994) and *Charlotte's Vow* (Beach Holme, 2000). She has published poems, newspaper articles and songs and belongs to a story-telling circle. She lives in Nanaimo, BC.

OTHER RAINCOAST YA FICTION:

*Spitfire* by Ann Goldring
1-55192-490-0 $9.95 CDN $6.95 US

*Wishing Star Summer* by Beryl Young
1-55192-450-1 $9.95 CDN $6.95 US

*The Accomplice* by Norma Charles
1-55192-430-7 $9.95 CDN $6.95 US

*Cat's Eye Corner* by Terry Griggs
1-55192-350-5 $9.95 CDN $6.95 US

*Dead Reckoning* by Julie Burtinshaw
1-55192-342-4 $9.95 CDN $6.95 US

*Raven's Flight* by Diane Silvey
1-55192-344-0 $9.95 CDN $6.95 US